Comments su
about her fii
Survive.

Diane Reid, Founder, Whispering Hope Ranch, Payson, AZ

"WOW! *9 Lives, I Will Survive*" deeply touched so many emotions and I am in awe of all that you have done, and of your wonderful family. Congratulations on capturing the story of Josh in such a remarkable way. Your work will surely help so many others who live similar lives. The photos of Josh are beautiful…what a fabulous, and unforgettable, smile. How wonderful! I can hardly wait to read the other books in the series.

Pam Sweetser, Executive Director Cultural Heritage Camps, Denver Colorado

"I sat down and read the entire first book, *9 Lives, I Will Survive,* in one day. It is truly an uplifting adoption story, but also very realistic. I love the "voice" you used, meaning Joshua's. That gives it credibility, plus an easy writing style to read - especially for adolescents and even younger. You have quite a story to tell and you are telling it so well! If all of that happened to YOUR Joshua, then he is some amazing kid for sure, and so are his parents! I mean, he really DOES have nine lives! It's great Jan - congratulations!"

Susan Fule, Former Social Worker and Mother of Two Boys, Albuquerque, NM

"My boys, ages 10 and 7, and I read, *9 Lives, I Will Survive,* aloud as a family and we loved it! Your style of writing, explaining technical or social work terms to kids was perfect for even my youngest son. Almost each time we read one of those parts he would say, 'I was just about to ask what that meant, and then it was explained to me.' You tell this story with tremendous tenderness, and bring to life Joshua's gentle spirit and his resilience. This is a lovely way to educate children about the foster care system, and the diversity of families. We can hardly wait for the next title in the trilogy to be released."

Cheri Scott, Adoptive Mother of Justin, AK

"I read the first book, *9 Lives, I Will Survive,* while my son and I were on the plane to Portland, finishing it before going to bed at our room in the hospital. What an enjoyable read! I think this book should appeal to a wide audience and we can't wait to read the next installment to see what happens in Joshua's life after being adopted."

9 Lives, Cat Tales

Jan Crossen

The second in a trilogy of fictional books inspired by my son, Joshua.

Dragonpublishing.net
Illinois

Published by
Dragonpublishing.net
www.dragonpublishing.net
Illinois

First printing.
Cover design by Shelley Baar

ISBN-13: 978-0-9798686-3-4
ISBN-10: 0-9798686-3-7

Printed in the United States of America

Dedications

I dedicate this book in loving memory to my parents, John and Aldine Crossen, and to my baby sister, Jill Crossen Allison. I love you all and miss you every day. It is also dedicated to my sister, Jonadine Crossen Randolph. I hope you know how much I love you.

Acknowledgements

Joshua, thank you so much for allowing me to use part of your story, to tell the fictional story of the young boy, Joshua, in this trilogy of books. Barbara, thank you for your support, and for your keen eye and perseverance in editing. Thank you, Linda, for your input and comments. Thanks to Paul at Dragonpublishing, for your help in bringing this second book in the series, into existence.

Meet the Author:
Jan Crossen, B.S., M.S.A.

Jan's interest in the welfare of children began years ago. As a high school teacher and coach, Jan was a mentor to many of her players. She has been a sponsor of children living in developing countries, and served as a court appointed surrogate parent for two young siblings in the Arizona foster care system.

Jan has always dreamed of creating her family through adoption. Her vision became a reality in 1999, when she adopted her son, Joshua. The three books in the *9 Lives Trilogy* were inspired by their lives together.

Introduction

My name is Joshua Radford Carson, and I'm adopted. I met my forever mom when I was eight. I'm black and my mom is white. Actually, I have two white mothers. Jamie Carson is my legal parent, and my second mom is Brooke Summer. I call her 'Momma B.' She's a veterinarian and my moms own an animal hospital together in Tucson, Arizona.

I have an older brother, Randall Jr. or R.J., and a baby sister named Amanda May. Unlike most brothers and sisters, we don't live together.

My birth mother, DeShona, drank alcohol while she was pregnant with me. She and my dad, Randall Radford Sr., had a lot of problems and weren't able to take care of us.

We were taken from their home and went to live with my aunt and uncle. It turned out that we weren't safe living with my Aunt Suzette and Uncle Joey. R.J., Amanda, and I had to split up. We each went to live in different homes with different families.

Amanda was immediately adopted, so she went to live with her new forever family. R.J. and I were put into two different foster homes. For a couple of years, I lived with a really nice woman named LaTisha Owens, and her family of foster and adopted kids.

Then I met my forever moms. Now our adoption is final and I have a new name, a forever family, and even my own bedroom in our new home. This fresh start was the beginning of some pretty tight experiences. I'm going to tell you about some of them.

Chapter 1

Meeting Alexi

"Come on, Mom," I pleaded, "Can we go now, please?"

"Honey, we can't check in until 9:00 a.m., and it's only 7:30 a.m. now," she said. "It will only take us twenty minutes to get to the bus stop where you'll meet the other kids and you'll all ride together to the YMCA Camp. You have about an hour before we need to leave. Did you get enough breakfast? Would you like some more toast?"

"No, thank you," I said, "I'm too excited to eat or do much of anything else. I just want to go to camp."

It was summertime, and I was scheduled to spend a week at the YMCA overnight camp. The night before camp, Mom had helped me pack my suitcase, backpack, and gear.

"Honey, do you want to take these shorts and jeans?" she asked, holding up four pairs of shorts and two pairs of old jeans.

"Yes, please," I answered.

"Why don't you grab a couple of sweatshirts, and I'll get your underwear and pajamas?"

"How many is a couple?"

"Two."

I selected my red hoodie and my navy blue pullover sweatshirts.

"All set, Mom."

"Josh, make sure you have your toothbrush and toothpaste, and here's a washcloth, towel, and soap."

"OK," I said, as I headed to the bathroom to get the items. I wasn't planning to use them, however. Whoever heard of brushing your teeth and taking a bath when you're camping?

At 8:30 a.m. we loaded the car and headed downtown to the YMCA building. There were at least two hundred kids and parents already there. We checked in at the registration table, and then sat down on the sidewalk to wait for the bus that would take us to the mountain camp.

"Excuse me, young man; are you going to camp this week?" a woman asked me.

"Yes, ma'am," I smiled, showing a lot of teeth. "I sure am!"

"Oh, great," she said. "I want you to meet my son, Alexi. He's going to camp too."

"Hi, I'm Josh."

Alexi and I shook hands and bumped fists.

"Alexi is from Russia," the woman said. "I recently adopted him, and he's only been in the United States for a few weeks. He doesn't know much English yet."

"I'm adopted too!" I said. "This is my mom." I pointed towards my mom and our mothers shook hands.

"Josh, I was wondering if you'd pal around with Alexi while he's at camp this week? I'm sure that he'd relax and have a much better time if he had a friend by his side."

"Sure," I said.

Alexi and I began communicating using hand and body motions. Sometimes we understood each other, but most of the time we just laughed as we tried to guess what the other kid was trying to say.

"May I have your attention please?" The YMCA leader said, using a loudspeaker system. "It's time for all campers to get on the buses."

"Have a great time, Honey, I'll see you in a week," Mom said as she kissed me.

Alexi said goodbye to his mom and we boarded the bus together.

"Find a seat, kids," the bus driver said, "We have plenty of room for everybody. Just in case you need it, we have a restroom in the back of the bus."

Alexi and I found two seats near the middle of the bus and sat down together. I waved once more to Mom from the window. We made the sign for "I love you" in sign language. Mom blew me a kiss, which I pretended to catch. I sent her a kiss too as the bus began to move. That was one of the routines we did whenever Mom tucked me in at night, or when we said 'good-bye.'

The bus was much nicer than any bus I had ever ridden. There were only two seats in each row, and they tilted back like my mom's Lazy-Boy recliner.

"Want some of my Cheese Doodles, Alexi?" I asked as we headed out of the parking lot and picked up speed.

Alexi gave me a puzzled look until I showed him the bag of snacks. He broke into a grin and pulled out his package of trail mix. We shared our snacks and began our friendship.

It was a long two-hour ride to Y-Camp. Everyone was pretty rowdy. We sang, told jokes and made a lot of noise. Everyone was excited.

Finally, we turned off the main road onto the Y-Camp driveway. The driver slowed the bus to about 15 miles per hour. The tires crunched on the gravel, as if they were eating the new stones on the road.

"Smell that fresh air," I said as I inhaled the scent of the Ponderosa Pine trees.

Alexi closed his eyes and took a deep breath of air. He smiled and nodded with pleasure.

In front of us was a dark green building with double, screened doors. Large, black screens covered the windows to let in the fresh, mountain air. This building would be our main meeting place during our week at camp.

Two by two, we paraded off the bus and went inside to the dining area. Sitting down at long picnic tables, we turned our attention to the camp counselors.

Dressed in navy blue shorts and green polo shirts, they looked over the campers with quiet confidence. Y-Camp was co-ed, which means boys and girls were there at the same time. The laughter and giggles slowly died down as a tall, white man, with a whistle around his neck, walked confidently to the front of the room.

Jan Crossen

Chapter 2

Y-Mountain Camp

"Welcome to the Y-Mountain Camp," the camp director said. "We're going to have a wonderful and fun week together."

Everyone clapped and cheered in agreement.

"Let's get things started. My name is John Hart, and I'm the camp director. This building is the Mess Hall, and we'll eat our meals here. There are 10 cabins for boys and an equal number for the girls," he said. "Each cabin has a counselor who is in charge of the campers in that bunk-house. When I call your name, the counselor in charge of your cabin will raise his or her arm high up in the air. Please go stand beside your counselor. Any questions?"

Nobody had a question. The director began calling the girls' names. He assigned each one to a cabin and counselor.

"The girls and their counselors are excused from the Mess Hall," the director said. "Now, I'll read the cabin assignments for the boys."

Alexi was assigned to a different cabin than the one I was in. He and I went to talk with the camp director and explained his situation.

"Hello, I am Alexi from Russia, I no speak English very good yet," he said.

"Would you please put Alexi in my cabin so that he can be with a friend?" I asked.

Mr. Hart thought that was a great idea so he reassigned Alexi to my cabin.

"Campers, follow your counselors to your cabins," the director said.

"We'll see you all back here for lunch. You'll hear the food bell ring in about an hour."

My counselor was a black guy named Hermie J. Flick. He was a big guy who wore his hair in corn-rows.

We followed Herm to our cabin, picked out our bunks, and put away our gear.

"Bongggg, Bongggg, Bongggg, Bongggg." A loud bell sounded, signaling that it was time for lunch.

"Race you to the Mess Hall," I said to Alexi and then sprinted in the direction of the sound.

Alexi broke into a run and was by my side every step of the way. We arrived at the front door smiling and panting for air. Sitting at our assigned tables, we waited for our turn at the buffet.

For lunch, I picked two fat and juicy Ballpark hot dogs. They were glistening with moisture as I stuck them with my fork and put them on my plate. I added a drop of Catsup and two perfectly toasted buns, and my Ballparks were ready to eat. I topped off my meal with a grape Popsicle.

Two of the girl counselors took the floor at the front of the room. One was the most beautiful black girl

I'd ever seen in my life. I immediately had a crush on her.

She was probably 20 years old, thin and about 5'10" tall. Her black hair was straight and hung to her shoulders. She had deep brown eyes and was really pretty.

The other girl was a perky, little, blonde, white girl. I couldn't help smiling every time she looked at me. She walked with a bounce and you could tell she was fun to be around.

These counselors taught us some funny songs with hand and arm motions. One was called, 'Boa Constrictor.' It went like this:

(chorus)
I'm being eaten by a boa constrictor,
a boa constrictor,
a boa constrictor,
I'm being eaten by a boa constrictor,
Oh, no, it's nibbling at my toe.

I'm being eaten by a boa constrictor,
a boa constrictor,
a boa constrictor,
I'm being eaten by a boa constrictor,
Oh, gee, he's up to my knee.

I'm being eaten by a boa constrictor,
a boa constrictor,
a boa constrictor,
I'm being eaten by a boa constrictor,
Oh, my, he's wrapping 'round my thigh.

The song goes on and ends with…Nah; I'm not going to tell you how it ends. You'll have to go to camp and learn that song for yourself.

After singing we listened as our camp director told us about the activities we would get to do over the next week.

"An activity schedule is posted outside of the Mess Hall on the bulletin-board," he said. "You'll each have a chance to swim in our outdoor pool, go horseback riding and hiking on the mountain trails, play soccer, tetherball, ping-pong, basketball and volleyball. And, finally, we'll have a camp dance on the last night before you all return home."

A thunderous applause erupted from the crowd of listeners. I covered my ears with my hands. The kids made way too much noise for me. It hurt my ears.

The director said, "In your crafts classes you'll make lanyards and sit-upons. You can use your sit-upons every night at your private cabin campfires."

I really liked craft classes. Alexi and I went to crafts the next morning after breakfast.

"You're very good with your hands, Joshua," the crafts lady said.

"Thanks," I said. "I like making things. I've already finished my sit-upon." I showed her my newspaper pillow. "I made it first thing this morning."

"That's great, Josh," she said. "Would you like to be my assistant and help the other campers with their projects?"

"Sure, can I help Alexi make his sit-upon?"

"You bet. Let me know if you need any more supplies."

Alexi and I trotted over to the columns of newsprint that were stacked on the floor. He selected his supplies, and I showed him how to weave them into a cushion. By the time the class was over Alexi was ready for the evening campfire.

Chapter 3

The Campfire

Alexi and I played basketball after dinner so we were always tired and hungry in the evenings. Herm was a miracle worker and managed to get a pack or two of marshmallows and hot dogs for us to roast at our campfire.

Each cabin had its own spot for the nightly events. Herm would light our fire right after our recreation time ended at 8:00 p.m. Then eight happy and dirty kids would eagerly huddle around the flames.

"Tube steaks taste better when they're cooked over a campfire," Herm would say every night.

That was our cue to grab a stick and a wiener and start roasting.

Herm called hot dogs, tube steaks. He said, "It makes them sound more expensive."

At night, we'd usually talk about what happened that day. Then Herm would play his guitar and we'd sing songs. You could tell that Alexi liked the music. He usually drummed softly on a hollow stump.

"Nice beat, Alexi," I said listening to him tap out the beat on the log. Trying to make him understand, I nodded my head to the beat and joined in the drumming. Alexi smiled and pounded even harder on his wooden drum.

Sometimes Herm would tell us scary stories. Alexi wasn't scared because he didn't understand much of what Herm was saying. He would watch our reactions though and try to get a feel for what was happening in the stories.

One night Herm was telling us about the time his jeep broke down in the desert far away from Tucson.

"It was a cool and quiet Sunday night. The fall moon was full and it shined brightly on the two lane road ahead," Herm began his story. "I had spent a long weekend visiting my folks in Sedona, Arizona. I was alone in my jeep and headed back to college at the University of Arizona. I was running late, so I decided to take a short cut back to school. "

We sat motionless and listened to his words.

"My engine sputtered, choked, and died." He made the sounds of the dying engine. "The jeep slowly drifted to a stop along the side of the road. I realized too late that I was out of gas and I was stranded. I looked around and there were no other cars in sight. I was easily 20 miles from the nearest little town. I could clearly see the desert landscape all around me."

Herm used his arms and body to act out the scene.

"Giant saguaro cacti were silhouetted against the night sky like an army of soldiers standing at attention."

Herm paused and slowly looked each of us in the eye.

"Suddenly, there was a loud scream," his voice quickened and his eyes grew large with alarm. "I heard the scream again. I could tell that the sound was coming towards me. I looked around, anxious to know what was going on."

I glanced nervously at Alexi, and then quickly back at Herm.

"Whamp, whamp, whamp, whamp."

I heard a sound that I didn't recognize.

"Whamp, whamp, whamp, whamp."

A dark shadow came directly at me. It was coming from above my head and was now just ten feet away. Ducking for cover, I dove under my jeep."

All eight of us were leaning forward with our eyes wide open. Alexi could sense the tension in the story and he sat perfectly still.

"A huge bird swooped to the road in front of my jeep. It snatched a small rodent from the ground, and effortlessly carried the prey in his deadly sharp talons."

With dramatic arm movements Herm mimicked the behavior of the large predator bird. Our eyes followed his every movement.

"It was a Great Horned Owl, hunting for food. He had captured his meal, and I was safe," Herm said.

"I sighed and chuckled with relief." Relieved, I laughed nervously and readjusted my seat.

"The night was once again peaceful. Off in the distance I saw headlights. I stood in the road ready to flag down the approaching driver."

I looked at Alexi and smiled, confident now that the story would soon have a happy ending.

"An awesome, red, 1986 Corvette Stingray zipped around the curve in the road. The convertible top was down, and a very attractive white woman, sat behind the wheel. She was traveling alone, and I waved my arms signaling for her to stop. She glanced at me, but didn't slow down. Her engine roared as she sped away."

I shook my head in disbelief. Why would anyone leave Herm stranded in the desert alone at night? That woman must have known that Herm needed help. What was her problem? Was she afraid of him? Was it because he was a big guy? A black man?

"I couldn't believe that she didn't stop to help me," Herm said. "I shook my head and dropped my waving arms."

I moved uneasily on my sit-upon. I wondered what would happen next, and how Herm would get out of this situation.

"There was a rustling in the bushes, and I held my breath to listen more clearly," Herm said.

"Rattttttttttttttttttttttttttttttttttttle,

Rattttttttttttttttttttttttttttttttttttttttle… It was the distinct rattle of a vibrating snake," he whispered.

"Rattttttttttttttttttttttttttttttttttttttle,

Rattttttttttttttttttttttttttttttttttttttttttle… The snake sent his warning message once again…"

I held my breath and sat perfectly still as I waited for Herm to continue his story. Just then a single trumpet broke the tension and the spell that had surrounded our campfire. A camp bugle sounding "Taps" interrupted Herm's story.

"Da-da-daaaaaaaaaaaaaaaaaaaaaaaaaaaaaaaaaaaa,

Da-da-daaaaaaaaaaaaaaaaaaaaaaaaaaaaaaaaaaaaa,

Da-da-daaaaaaaaaa,

Da-da-daaaaaaaaaa,

Da-da-daaaaaaaaaa,

Da-da-daaaaaaaaaa,

Da-da-daaaaaaaaa,
Da-da-daaaaaaaaaaaaaaaaaaaaaaaaa."

The horn signaled that it was time to drown our fire and head for our bunks. In thirty minutes it would be time for lights out.

"Sorry guys, that's it for tonight," Herm said.

"Ahhhhhhhhhhhh, come on, Herm, finish the story," we pleaded.

"To be continued…You know the rules. Maybe we'll finish it tomorrow night. Now hit the can and then get into your bunks," he said.

We slowly got to our feet and stretched. Herm poured a bucket of water on the fire. With the hiss of a snake and a puff of black smoke, the campfire was out.

We picked up our gear and turned towards the restroom and shower cabin. That's when we heard the warning rattle of a nearby snake.

"Rattttttttttttttttttttttttttttttttttttle;
Rattttttttttttttttttttttttttttttttttttttle;"

"Shhhh!" Herm said. "Freeze!"

We stopped in our tracks, unable to identify the source of the noise.

"Rattttttttttttttttttttttttttttttttttttle;
Rattttttttttttttttttttttttttttttttttttttttle," it sounded again.

We held our breath and watched as a 6 foot long rattlesnake cross the path that lead to our cabin. It slithered quickly into the woods.

"Gospodi!" Alexi exclaimed once the serpent had left our immediate area.

"Gospodi!" he repeated shaking his head, his eyes huge with fright.

"What does that mean?" I asked.

"I don't speak Russian, but I think maybe Alexi was saying, 'Oh my God!'" Herm said.

"I can't believe you were just talking about a rattlesnake and one showed up in our camp!" I said. "Oh, my God is right!"

"Watch carefully where you're walking," Herm said. "And make heavy footsteps. Snakes feel the vibrations and should stay out of our way. Let's go!"

We quickly hit the restroom and were safely in our beds within record time. Nobody wanted to risk being out and about with poisonous reptiles in the area.

The next morning camp was buzzing with stories of our reptile visitor. Some kids didn't believe that we had a rattlesnake in our camp. But we knew that what we saw and heard was no campfire story.

Jan Crossen

Chapter 4

Call Me 'Cat'

On the third day of camp I got to spend some time alone with Herm. We started talking and I found out we had a lot in common.

Herm had a scar near his left eye. He said he got it when he was a little kid. He said that he was at his uncle's house. The grown-ups were inside and he was outside playing. He saw a wooden ladder leaning up against the garage. He decided to climb it.

Herm got almost to the top when he lost his balance. He fell over backwards, landing on the gravel driveway. The force of the fall knocked the breath out of his lungs. The heavy ladder fell on top of him.

"I must have smashed my face against a rock because blood started pouring out of me," he said. "I couldn't breathe. I couldn't see because there was blood all over my eye."

"Ewwww!" I said.

"Finally, I was able to scream for my mom. She heard me and ran outside."

"Then what?"

"Mom tossed that ladder off of me like it was no heavier than a baseball bat," Herm said laughing. "She held a cold, wet rag to my head and took me to the hospital emergency room. I ended up having eight stitches right next to my eye."

"Wow, I bet that hurt," I said.

"Yeah. And the doctor said I was lucky I didn't poke my eye out. If I had landed on that stone any differently, I'd be staring at you through a glass eye for sure."

We sat quietly for a while, tossing little pebbles at a fallen tree.

"I had some scary accidents too," I said. "Want to hear about them?"

"Sure."

I told Herm about being born before I was ready, and how I almost died as a baby. He heard about my month long coma. I said that the doctor told my foster mom to plan my funeral, because I was probably going to die.

I showed him the scar on the back of my head. I explained how I got it while I was in the coma in the hospital.

I told Herm how my adopted mom, Jamie, explained my bald scar. She said that it was really an "angel kiss." Mom said that, "the angel kissed me to wake me up so that I could be her son, and she could be my forever mom."

Finally, I told him about my near drowning. I told him how my Guardian Angel, and my foster brother, Jabar, and my moms, and the EMTs all helped to save my life.

"Man, you're a miracle kid!" Herm said. "You're like a lucky cat, man, a cat with nine lives."

I nodded my agreement.

"You should have a nickname," Herm said. "You're a cool kid and one very lucky cat. I think I'll call you 'Cat.' Is that OK with you?"

"That'd be tight," I said, beaming with pride. "Thanks, man."

We bumped fists and shook hands. From that night on, Herm and my cabin friends called me 'Cat.' I started telling other kids to use my nickname, too.

"Call me 'Cat,'" I'd say with a smile.

Chapter 5

Coming Home

While I was away at camp, my parents had been busy shopping for me. I didn't know about the surprises my moms had waiting for me at home.

"Josh needs new clothes," Mom said to Brooke as they entered the 'Boys' section of the Target store. "He needs shirts, jeans, shorts, underwear, shoes, pajamas…"

"This is going to be fun!" Brooke said with a laugh. "And expensive."

"It sure is!" Mom said. "Let's get started. He wears a size 6 slim jean."

"The jeans are right here," Brooke said. She began sorting through the sizes.

"Let's get three pair, two blue and one black."

"OK," Mom said, "You get those while I pick up some shorts. I have a feeling this will be one shopping trip we'll never forget!"

My parents bought me an entire new wardrobe that day. And that was just the beginning.

In addition to the new clothes, my folks had decorated my room with all sorts of cool things. They were excited to see my reaction to all of their efforts while I was away at summer camp.

Mom met the bus from camp and I greeted her with a jump-hug. During the drive home I told her the campfire and rattlesnake story. I also told her about my new nickname.

"Well, Honey, the name 'Cat' does seem to fit," she said. "And you know how much we love cats around our house. I'm sure Brooke will think it's a great nickname too."

We pulled into our garage and I jumped out of the Subaru.

"Cat-Honey, would you please drop your dirty clothes at the laundry room? Then take the rest of your things to your room?" Mom asked.

I dumped my dirty clothes on the floor of the laundry room. I started calling for my other mother.

"Momma B, I'm home!" I said.

"I'm in your room, Josh," Momma B yelled back.

I walked into my bedroom and couldn't believe my eyes. Momma B was sitting on the bed waiting for me. She jumped to her feet and greeted me with a hug and kiss. My mom appeared in my bedroom door. She smiled at me.

"Oh, my gosh," I said. "Check out my room. I love it! Look at this new dresser. It's blue. And that's a new blanket on my bed!"

I dove onto the bed and laughed as I wrapped myself in the warm blue comforter.

"How do you like your pillow, Josh?" Momma B asked, holding up a pillow with Bugs Bunny's face.

His big toothy grin smiled at me and his long gray ears poked out from the side of the blue fabric. Bugs Bunny has always been my favorite cartoon character.

"He's tight!" I said taking the pillow from her.

"And here's a Bugs Bunny baseball cap for you too," Mom said handing me the blue cap.

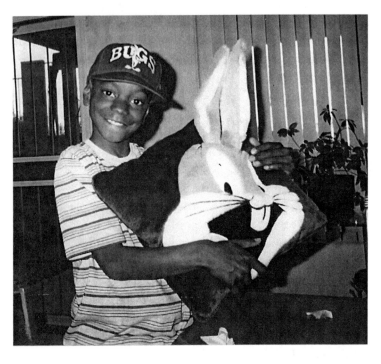

I looked around my room. My walls had been painted, and were decorated with posters and pictures of black people.

"Do you know who any of these people are?" Mom asked.

"Sure, that's Martin Luther King, Jr., and that's Michael Jordan," I said pointing to their correct images.

"Very good," she said. "Do you know any of the others?"

I shook my head from side to side, "No."

"This is Arthur Ashe," Mom said. "He was a famous tennis player. And over here is Frank Robinson. He was my favorite professional baseball player when I was a kid. He wore uniform #20 and played for the Cincinnati Reds."

I walked over to examine the faces on my walls.

"Hey, Josh, do you know who this handsome guy is?" Mom asked.

"No, but he's a football player," I said.

"You're right, that's Lynn Swan," Mom said. "He played for the World Champion Pittsburgh Steelers. I've always had a big crush on him."

"Ah, Mom."

"Well, it's true," she said.

"I bet that before long you'll be able to name the other famous African Americans on this poster," Momma B said, referring to a poster.

"Who are they?" I asked.

"I only recognize a few of them," she said. "Here's a guide to tell us who's who," she said, handing me a paper.

"You know how I love American history," Mom said. "It'll be fun learning more about these important people."

Then I spotted four photographs of some children. I walked over to get a better look. They were black and white pictures of some kids who were playing in a park.

One photo had five young girls playing together on a swing set. Three of the girls were black and two were white. The next photo had the same kids hanging on a 'Jungle Jim' set.

There was a photo of a young black boy standing on the sidewalk. He was holding a string that was tied to a helium balloon.

The last picture was of three white girls standing in front of a wall. The girl in the middle had a smirk on her face, while her friends covered their mouths to keep from giggling.

"Do you have a favorite photo?" Mom asked.

"Yes, ma'am, I like this one the best," I said pointing to the three girls.

"I like that one, too," she said. "It's called 'The Secret.' Do you think the girl in the middle has a secret?"

"Yes, ma'am," I said. "And unlike me, she's not telling."

We laughed because we all know that I am not good at keeping a secret.

"Josh, you might want to check out your closet," Momma B said.

I opened my closet door. "Wow!"

I saw all of the new clothes and shoes. I dropped to the floor and grabbed a brand new pair of basketball shoes. I smelled them and then held them up in the air. I love to smell things. These shoes smelled brand new! "These are tight!" I said. "Thank you!"

I put them back in their box and picked up a pair of brown shoes with laces on the top.

"Those are for school," Momma B said.

I smelled them too and held them up to admire. Next I examined a pair of black loafers.

"What are these?" I asked.

"They're called loafers," Mom said. "You just slide your feet into them like slippers. With loafers you don't have to worry about tying any laces."

"Sweet."

The leather smelled great. I knew that I'd like wearing them. Then I spotted my dress shoes.

"Wow, look at these," I said. "They're so shiny that I can see myself!"

I love shiny things and these shoes were polished dress shoes. They were black and for special occasions. I put them on and strutted like a proud rooster into the kitchen. There I danced all over the tile floor.

My folks followed me into the kitchen and clapped for me as I showed them my fancy footwork.

"You get your dancing ability from your mom," Momma B said, laughing.

"May I try on my new clothes?"

"Sure, but how about taking a bath first?" Mom said, "You have at least an acre of camp dirt on you."

I ran to the bathroom and started running water in the tub. Within fifteen minutes I was in and out of the bath. I was ready to try on my new threads.

I'd never had so many new clothes and shoes before. The state of Arizona provides each kid in foster care a little money to buy clothes and shoes each year. It isn't much money, so most foster parents go to thrift stores to get clothes for their foster kids. I was thrilled to have brand new clothes that nobody else had ever worn before.

I ran to Mom and gave her a jump-hug. Then I gave Momma B a jump-hug too. "Thank you both so much for my room and new clothes and my shoes." I said.

"You're welcome, Honey, it's our pleasure," they said.

"Thank you for 'dopting me."

"It's our pleasure. Thanks for being our son, Joshie, we love you very much."

"I love you too!" I said with a smile and skipped down the hall.

Chapter 6

Mom's School

"Honey, I need to talk with you," Mom said. "Please come over here and sit by me."

Joining her on the couch, I looked into her face. Mom looked serious.

"I know that you've been angry because you were hurt by adults in the past. And nobody blames you for what happened, or for being mad at the grown-ups in your life. I'd be angry too."

She had my full attention.

"But because of your anger, Josh, you haven't been able to focus much on your school work. For the past three years, your teachers have been helping you learn to handle your emotions. They've been trying to teach you to have more appropriate behaviors. Do you understand what I've said so far?"

I nodded that I understood, "Yes, ma'am."

"Because you've been dealing with your anger, you're behind in what you should have already learned in school. Does that make sense?"

Again I nodded my head, "Yes, ma'am."

"Good. I was thinking that we should take advantage of your summer vacation. I think that we should work together on your schoolwork. We could work for about an hour every day. I'm hoping that we can get you caught up a little. "Will you do that with me? Will you work with me to help you get caught up with your school work?"

"OK," I said.

"Thank you, Josh. I'll get some workbooks and we'll start this week. I'd like to ask you to do some things. You may already know how to do some of them. That way I can figure out where we should start. Is that OK?"

"Uh, huh, I mean, yes ma'am."

"OK," she smiled, "I don't mean to bore or insult you, but I need to find out what you already know and what you don't know. Can you say the alphabet for me?"

"Sure!" I said, and quickly rattled off the letters.

"Good, now do you know which letters are called vowels?"

"Uhmmmm…I'm not sure."

"Let's look at your name."

Mom printed 'J-O-S-H-U-A' on a piece of paper.

"One example of a vowel would be the letter 'A,'" she said.

"Oh, yeah," I said. "I remember now, A, E, I, O, U."

"That's right. So what are the other vowels in your name?"

"O and U."

"Excellent. Have you learned about 'Phonics'?"

"I don't think so, what's a Phonic?"

Jan Crossen

"Well, it's a great way to help you read and learn how to pronounce new words. You start learning Phonics by hearing the different sounds that vowels and consonants make. Do you know what a consonant is?"

"Those are the letters that aren't vowels."

"Right. Can you name the consonants in your name?"

"J, S, and H," I said pointing to each letter in my name.

"Exactly. Do you know the other sounds that each vowel can make?" Mom asked. "Let's look at the word 'skate.'"

Mom wrote the word, 'skate,' on the paper.

"Do you see the 'e' on the end of the word?"

"Yes, ma'am."

"Well that 'e' on the end of this word tells you that the vowel in front of it, says its own name. What is the vowel in front of the 'e'?"

"It's the letter 'a'."

"Exactly, so for this word the 'a' says its own name. We say, 'skate'. Do you hear the 'A' sound in the word skate?"

"Yes, ma'am."

"When a vowel says its own name, we call that a long vowel sound. Like the letter 'a' in skate. OK?"

"I think so."

Mom wrote some different words on the paper. We practiced words that had long vowel sounds. Each word had the letter 'e' on the end of it. I started getting bored.

"OK, that's all for today, Joshie. School's out for the day. Great job. Now let's go shoot some hoops."

46

Mom and I had a good time making baskets. I almost beat her at the game of "Horse." One of these days I know that I'll beat her. I'm going to practice my shooting until I do!

Later that night my parents were sitting at the kitchen table talking. I was already in bed, but still awake. I could hear their voices, but I couldn't make out any of the words.

"So how did the school lesson go today?" Brooke asked.

"Oh, Brooke," Mom said, "I'm shocked at how low Josh's reading level is. He's nine years old and in the third grade. He can barely read even the easiest words. He knows his alphabet and a little bit about Phonics. This is going to be much harder than I had planned. It's going to take a lot of hard work for him to catch up to his age and grade level."

Mom and I worked together every day that summer, even though I didn't like it very much. Whenever I'd finish a workbook, my folks always made a big deal out of what I had accomplished.

"DAH-da-da-DAH! Ladies and germs, I mean gentlemen," Mom said.

She was pretending to be an announcer standing in front of a large crowd.

"I'd like to call your attention to the outstanding achievement of Mr. Joshua Carson. Today he successfully completed another workbook. Mr. Carson, would you please step forward?"

My parents clapped and cheered as they presented me with an achievement award certificate. I liked getting my awards and kept them in a three ring binder.

When I got better at phonics, my parents asked me to read to one of them for half an hour every day. Mom usually picked out most of my books. They were often about famous black people, or black history, or black families. My folks didn't want me to forget that I was an African American.

Chapter 7

Discovering Girls

I had my first girlfriend in the third grade. She was white and had pretty blonde hair that she wore in a ponytail. Her name was Peggy, and I called her Pretty Peggy. She wasn't in my classroom, but we played tag during recess.

"Class," my teacher, Mrs. Jones, said. "Tomorrow is Grandparents' Visitation day. There will be many visitors at our school. Joshua's grandparents are the only guests from our classroom that will be visiting this year. This is a very special occasion. I've ordered a flower for you, Joshua, to give to your grandmother. I expect everyone to be on his or her best behavior tomorrow."

"Thank you, Mrs. Jones," I said. "I'm sure that Grandma will like the flower."

"I'm sure she will too," Mrs. Jones said. "Your grandparents will arrive at 10:30 a.m. Josh, you will meet them at the principal's office and escort them to our room."

I listened carefully to my teacher's instructions.

"You will introduce them to the class, and show them your desk. You may give them a tour of the room. Be sure to point out your own work, which is on display on the walls."

"O.K.," I said with a smile.

"Then Joshua, you are to take your guests to the cafeteria. They will be eating lunch with you. You should lead them through the cafeteria line. After you finish your meal, your grandparents' visit will be over. They will leave the school. You are to come back to class for our afternoon work as usual. OK?"

I nodded that I understood.

At 10:15 a.m. the next day, Mrs. Jones sent me to the office to pick up the flower that she had ordered for my Grandmother. The flower turned out to be a red carnation and it had something called 'Baby's Breath' with it. 'Baby's Breath' is a bunch of little dainty white flowers all on the same stem.

I wanted to impress my girlfriend, Peggy, so I ran quickly down the hallway to her classroom door. Standing outside, I waved to get her attention.

"May I please use the restroom?" Peggy asked her teacher.

The teacher gave her approval, and Peggy stepped into the hallway.

"Hi, Pretty Peggy," I said smiling. "This flower is for you," I said, handing her the red carnation.

Her deep, blue eyes lit up with surprise. "Thank you so much, Joshua!"

Then Peggy kissed my cheek. I blushed. She returned to her classroom and beamed with joy as she proudly showed everyone her red flower.

Feeling very pleased with myself, I skipped down the hall to the principal's office where I would meet my mom's folks. My grandparents were just walking into the building. I handed the 'Baby's Breath' to Grandma.

"This flower is for you, Grandma," I said, and gave her a hug.

"Well, thank you, Joshua," my grandmother said. "How lovely."

I hugged my grandpa too, and then walked my guests to my classroom. I held the door as they walked in.

"Mrs. Jones, this is 'Grandma' and this is 'Grandpa,'" I said.

The grown-ups shook hands.

"Everybody, these are my grandparents," I told my classmates.

Nobody seemed surprised that my grandparents were white. They all knew that I was adopted and that my mom was white.

"This is my seat," I said, pointing to the desk closest to Mrs. Jones' desk.

"Come here," I said, pulling on Grandma's arm. "I want to show you my work on the walls."

My grandfather followed us to the back corner of the room.

"This is my drawing," I said. "It's a picture of me. I drew it myself."

"That's a good likeness, Josh," Grandpa said. "It really looks like you."

He patted me on the back.

"It really does, Joshua," Grandma said. "I wish that I could draw that well."

"The only thing I can draw is flies in the summertime," Grandpa said, laughing.

I looked at him confused. Grandpa likes to tell jokes, but if that was a joke, I didn't get it.

"Joshua, it's time for you to escort your guests to the lunchroom," Mrs. Jones said. "Thank you so much for visiting us today. It meant a great deal to Joshua."

"Goodbye," my classmates said as they waved.

I took my grandmother's hand and led the way to the cafeteria. We had pizza for lunch. I handed each of my grandparents a tray and then took one for myself. We were each handed a plate with a slice of pepperoni pizza, some salad, and a container of applesauce.

"Let's sit over here," I said, pointing to my usual table.

We sat down and I immediately began removing the pepperoni from my pizza.

"Why, Josh, don't you like the meat?" Grandpa asked.

"No, sir" I said. "Would you like it?"

I offered it to him with my bare hands.

"No, thank you," Grandpa said.

"May I please put it on your plate then?" I asked.

He nodded and I deposited my pepperoni onto his tray.

I gobbled down my pizza. I really only liked the bread. I didn't touch my salad or my applesauce.

"May I please be excused?" I asked.

"Are you finished eating?" Grandpa said. "There's still a lot of food on your plate?"

"Yes, I'm full. May I please be excused?"

"Well, OK…" Grandma said.

She wondered what I was planning. I stood up from my seat and gave each of them a quick kiss on the cheek.

"Thanks for coming," I said. Leaving my tray on the table, I ran outside to play tag with Peggy. My grandparents laughed.

"No wonder that boy is so thin," my grandmother said. "He doesn't eat very much."

"No, but he has good taste in girls," Grandpa said in my defense. "That blonde with the pony tail is a real pretty little girl."

They finished their meals, took the empty trays and dishes to the drop off counter. Within minutes, they had left the school.

That evening, Grandma and Grandpa called Mom on the phone. They had two phones so they could both talk to my mom at the same time. Mom wasn't too pleased when she found out that I had given Grandma only part of her flower.

"Joshua, what happened to the carnation today?" Mom asked.

"I gave it to my girlfriend, Pretty Peggy," I said. "Wasn't the flower supposed to be for your grandmother?"

"Yes, but Grandma still got a flower too."

Mom shook her head. She relayed what I had said into the phone.

"Oh, cut him a break," Grandma said to my mother. "He's only in the third grade. I thought it was cute."

"He's a pretty clever kid," Grandpa said. "To think of splitting the flowers between his girlfriend and his grandmother."

Mom was quiet as she listened to what was being said on the phone.

"I can't believe that Josh went outside to play tag," Mom said. "Leaving you sitting alone in the cafeteria."

"That boy's got good taste, Jamie," Grandpa said. "He'll be OK."

"You know," Grandma said to my mom, "Mrs. Jones told us that no child from her classroom has ever had grandparents visit before. Now that's a shame."

"It certainly is. Thank you for doing that for Josh," Mom said. "I'm sure that Joshua appreciated your visit."

And she was right, I did!

Jan Crossen

Chapter 8

Nightmares

Jan Crossen

"Mom!" I awoke with terror and cried out in the middle of the night.

"Mom!" I sounded a second, blood-curdling scream. Before the word was out of my mouth, the light was on and my mother was at my bedside.

"It's OK, Honey, I'm here," she assured me as she wrapped me in her arms. "Shhhhhhhh, shhhhhhhhh, you're safe now, Sweetheart, nobody's going to hurt you."

"He tried to kill me," I sobbed. "In my dream Uncle Joey was trying to shoot me with a pistol."

When I was younger I lived for a while with Uncle Joey and Aunt Suzette. My aunt was nice, but Uncle Joey was really mean. He was especially violent when he was drunk. He abused my brother and me, and I'm still really mad about what he did to me.

"Oh, Joshie, I'm so sorry. It's OK, Baby, you're safe now."

"Does Uncle Joey know where I am? Can he find me? Can he hurt me?"

"No, Josh, he doesn't have any idea where you are," Mom said, looking me in the eyes. "He'll never find you or hurt you again, I promise."

Mom was worried about the many weekly nightmares that I had. She and Momma B took me to a psychiatrist. That's a doctor who helps you when you're upset a lot. Mom asked him to help me.

"Hi, Joshua," he said. "I'm Doctor French."

The doctor shook my hand.

"Your mother has asked me to talk with you. We want to find some ways to help you feel better. I'd like you to step into this room so that we can talk for a while. Your moms will be waiting right here for you when we finish. OK?"

"OK," I said.

Mom had told me about Dr. French. She said that he would try and help me stop having nightmares. I was all for that.

"I'd like to ask you some questions, Joshua. Is that OK with you?"

"Yes."

"If I am going to help you, I need you to be honest with me. Will you do your best to tell me the truth?"

"Yes, sir."

Dr. French let me play with some dump trucks while we talked about my life. He asked me a lot of questions. He asked about my nightmares, my birth parents, Uncle Joey and Aunt Suzette. We played a long time together. When we were finished playing, he talked with my folks. I continued to play on the floor.

"Joshua has a diagnosis with a couple of areas of concern," he said. "He is ADHD which stands for Attention Deficit Hyperactivity Disorder. That means that he has difficulty focusing his attention and needs to move around frequently. We can help his ADHD with some prescription medications."

"You said 'a couple of areas of concern', what else is there?" Mom asked.

"He suffers from 'PTSD'. That stands for Post Traumatic Stress Disorder. It means that he remembers and relives the abuse from when he was much younger. The PTSD is causing his nightmares. He could continue to have those for quite some time."

"How do we help him?" Momma B asked.

"I'd suggest a type of treatment called play therapy. It would be good for him to work through his anger towards his uncle. There are a couple of places in town that work with young kids using play therapy," he said. He handed my mother a sheet of paper with the names and addresses of professionals who worked with kids.

"Good luck, Joshua," he said. "Goodbye."

Mom got me connected with a woman who did play therapy.

After several sessions of working with me, the therapist met with my folks.

"There is nothing else that I can do for Joshua," she told them. "He's being nice to the bad guys. He's serving coffee and donuts to them. I'm sorry, but I've done all that I can for him."

"What else can we do to help him?" Mom asked. "He's still angry and he's still acting out a lot at school and at home. He still has nightmares."

"I'm sorry, but I don't know what to tell you," the therapist said. "I wish I did." The therapist shook her head.

"Good luck," she said and walked away from us.

"We need to find additional therapy services for Josh," Momma B said. "He's not over his issues if he's still acting out."

"I agree," my mom said. "We'll keep looking for help. In the meantime, let's see what we can do to improve his self-esteem. Let's get him enrolled in some activities that will build his skills and confidence."

"That's a good idea," Momma B said. "And let's see what else we can do to promote his identity as an African American. I sure wish the Big Brothers and Big Sisters organization would find a black mentor for him. He's been on their waiting list for several months now. Having a positive black role model would really help him, I think."

"It sure would," Mom said.

Jan Crossen

Chapter 9

The Other Side

Mom asked LaTisha, my former foster mom, for the name of a good child therapist. She suggested a woman named Katy Wilson. My moms and I went together to our first meeting with Katy. She asked me a lot of questions and then let me play with the stuff in her toy box.

"It seems that Josh is very angry because of the neglect and abuse he suffered as a youngster," Katy told my parents. "He's insecure and desperate for attention, any kind of attention. It doesn't matter to him if people are praising or scolding, as long as they see him. He wants someone to know that he exists."

"We're working hard at improving his self-esteem," Mom said. "We praise him when he does positive things."

"It's difficult to reward his behaviors when he acts out, lies, and steals," Momma B said.

It's true that I did those things. I lied about stuff because I didn't want to get caught and be in trouble.

Then my parents would be mad at me and I'd have consequences. Sometimes I would lose my privileges and couldn't watch television, play with my Game Boy, or play my computer games.

I stole things because I wanted them. It didn't matter to me that they belonged to someone. I took things from my parents, my teachers, and other kids at school. I'd pick things up in stores, and even took things that I wanted from my parents' veterinary clinic. It was easy for me to steal things. I thought that I was getting away with it, but I usually got caught sooner or later.

"Perhaps Josh steals as a result of the neglect he experienced as a young child," Katy said.

"OK, but he has everything he needs now," Mom said. "How long will this go on? We have a rule, 'nothing comes into this house without my approval.' We have that rule because Josh is always showing up with toys, or office supplies, or other things that he's taken from someone. We make him return the item and apologize, but he just keeps stealing."

"And sometimes he's very defiant at home," Momma B said. "We know that older children who are adopted often have a 'honeymoon' period, a time when they are on their best behavior at home. Well, the honeymoon is definitely over for us."

"I wonder if Joshua is testing our love," Mom said. "Every day he pushes the limits to see if we are really committed to him."

"All of that is certainly possible. Joshua still isn't ready to trust the grown-ups in his life," Katy said. "That's going to take a lot of time and consistent parenting on your part."

"It bothers me that Joshua hugs people that he has just met," Mom said.

"Sometimes, I feel as though Brooke and I aren't really special to Josh. It's as though he'd go to anyone who treated him well, and made sure that he was fed, clothed, and entertained."

"Joshua may have a disability called Reactive Attachment Disorder or RAD,' Katy said.

"What does that mean?" Mom asked.

"Basically, it means that Joshua may not be capable of really bonding with anyone," Katy said. "It's very sad, but it does happen."

"Wow," Mom said.

The room was quiet for a while.

"Josh has been diagnosed with ADHD," Momma B said. "I understand that he has difficulty staying focused and sitting still, but what about the disruptions that he causes in class?"

"Josh's school decided that he needed to be in special education classes," Mom said. "His IQ is in the normal range, but he may have learning disabilities. The special education classes are smaller than the regular classrooms. And Josh gets more one-on-one attention than he would in a mainstream room. He's in a self-contained classroom because of his anger and emotional problems."

"EEEEaaaaaaaaaawwwwwwwwwwwwwwwww."
I was pleased with the loud noise that I made. I giggled at myself.

"Joshua, why did you do that just now?" Katy asked.

"I guess 'cause I felt like it."

"Do you make those noises in school?" Katy said.

66

"Sometimes."

"What happens when you do that?"

"My teacher says, 'Joshua, stop disrupting class,'" I said, mimicking my teacher's voice.

"But I like making weird noises. It makes the other kids laugh."

"So you enjoy being the class clown?" Katy asked.

"Yeah, it's fun."

"That brings up another issue," Mom said. "Josh claims to have a lot of friends, but he usually doesn't even know his classmates' first names. He doesn't bother to learn anyone's last name."

"And no one calls or invites him to do anything. His relationships are all very surface. It's really very sad," said Momma B.

"EEEEaaaaaaaawwwwwwwwwwwwwwwwwww," I wailed again.

"OK, Josh, no one is laughing here. I need you to stop making those noises," Mom said.

Katy and my folks continued talking.

"EEEaaaaaaaaawwwwwwwwwwwwwwwwwww."

"Joshua, that's not acceptable behavior. Take a time out in that corner," Mom said, pointing to a corner away from the toy box. "And leave all of the toys here."

Stomping across the room, I plopped down on the floor with a loud thud. I began picking at the carpet. It sounded to me like a cat sharpening its nails on a rug. I lifted my butt and legs off the floor with my arms. Then I'd let myself drop back onto the rug making a 'huff.' I did that several times, but the grownups ignored me. I got bored and lost interest. Closing my eyes, I took a catnap. I rested, but listened to every word that was being said about me.

"Joshua's teacher sends home notes about his behaviors," Mom said. Sometimes his teacher will call and ask me what he should do about him. Shoot, he's supposed to be the expert on dealing with kids who have emotional issues. I've suggested moving his desk right next to the teacher's desk, or moving him to the back of the room, far away from the other students. Nothing seems to work."

"Over the years, Joshua's teachers have tried a lot of different methods to correct his behaviors. They've taken recess away from him, given him detention, lectured him, suspended and threatened to expel him," Momma B said. "They've tried rewarding Josh with toys and food. Nothing makes an impact. He continues to disrupt the class. It's as though he doesn't care about anything."

"And it takes Josh a very long time to get his work done," Mom said.

"Special education teachers don't give much homework. One time I asked his teacher why Josh never had homework. I was told, 'He probably wouldn't do the homework anyway. Why should I cause another battle for the parents at home?'"

"If they do give an assignment, it's usually some sort of a project," Momma B said. "And Josh never finishes a project."

"That's true. And his teachers have told us that, even during class, he doesn't finished his work or turn it in. He just doesn't seem to care."

"Josh's teacher said that he tries to be the first student finished with his test papers," Momma B said.

"He apparently doesn't bother reading the directions or checking his answers. He just wants to hand his test in first."

"It's like he thinks it's all a game, and the person who finishes first wins," Mom said.

"Josh never studies for his quizzes or tests," Mom added. "We'll ask him about homework, projects, or tests, and he'll say that he doesn't have any."

"Then we see his report card and find out that he's just not doing his work," Momma B said. "He's busy acting out, trying to be funny, and socializing."

"Does Joshua express dreams for his future?" Katy asked.

"Oh, yes," Mom said. "But they aren't realistic. One day he wants to be a magician, the next day a businessman, and later that week he wants to be a veterinarian. It's fine that his goals change, but he doesn't seem to understand that he needs to study and do well in school in order to get into college."

"Let me recap," Katy said, "Joshua has a normal IQ and is in a self-contained classroom, which he disrupts frequently. He has outbursts in class and doesn't stop when he is asked. He enjoys the attention of being a class clown, thinks everyone is his friend, yet he doesn't have any close friends. Nobody calls to invite him to play. Is that correct so far?"

"Yes, and the fact that he tries to push our buttons in an effort to get attention," Mom said.

"Josh lies and steals and is defiant. He doesn't seem to be able to follow directions. It's as though he thinks the rules don't apply to him," Katy said.

"Exactly," Mom said.

"I'd like to discuss Joshua's behaviors with my supervisor. I'll see what we might be able to put into place to help all of you."

"Thank you," my folks said at the same time.

"Joshie, wake up, it's time to go now," Mom said.

"Huh? What?" I said, pretending to awaken from a deep sleep.

"It's time to go home now, Josh." Momma B said.

"OK," I said standing. I gave a big loud stretch. "Ahhhhhhhhhhhhhhhhhhhh, Ohhhhhhhhhhhhhhhhhh."

"See you next week, Joshua," Katy said. "Goodbye."

"Goodbye, Katy, thanks for letting me play with your toys," I said. I took hold of my mothers' hands, and we walked out the door.

Chapter 10

Helpful Ideas

Jan Crossen

At our next meeting, my therapist, Katy, told us about several suggestions that she had to help my family and me.

"You told me that Joshua recently had a physical examination, right?" Katy asked. "And that his physical health is fine?"

"Yes," Mom said.

"And Dr. French gave him an IQ test and a psychological evaluation," Katy said. "You said that Josh has a normal IQ, and that he has a diagnosis of PTSD and ADHD?"

"That's correct."

"OK, I just wanted to make sure. Is he taking any medications to help with his ADHD?"

"Yes, he's on two different medications," Mom answered.

"Do you think they are helping?"

72

"Yes, we noticed an immediate improvement when he started them. He isn't as combative now as he used to be." Momma B said.

"Good. I think that we should schedule a regular program of monthly weekend respite for Joshua," Katy said.

"What's a respite?" I asked.

"That's when you spend a weekend away from home. You have someone other than your parents taking care of you," Katy said. "It gives you and your moms a little break from each other."

"That sounds good," Momma B said. "Let's make it happen."

"It would be good if Josh had a black man to hang out with," Katy said. "What about enrolling him in a program like Big Brothers and Sisters?"

"He's already registered," Mom said. "He's been waiting for a match with an African American man for several months already."

"That's great, let's hope that he finds a match soon," Katy said. "In the meantime, I could schedule one of our interns to come out once a week and spend a couple of hours with Josh. They could shoot baskets or something. It wouldn't be a black male, but it would bring a male presence into his world. What do you say, Josh? Would you like to hang with one of our guys once a week?"

"That'd be tight," I said. "Excuse me, may I use the restroom?"

Katy pointed to the men's room door and away I went. "Since Josh has difficulty in social settings and in making friends, I'd like to invite him to participate in a weekend program that I run. It's called 'Saturday Group' and we spend three hours each week, working on social skills. We play games, eat lunch, and practice appropriate behaviors. At the end of the day, everyone gets a prize. It would be perfect for Josh."

"That sounds great," Momma B said, as I walked back into the room.

"Let's tell him about it now," Mom said.

Katy smiled and nodded, "Please do."

"Josh, you've been invited to join a group of kids that get together every Saturday. They play games and eat lunch together, and you'll even get a prize at the end of the day. Katy will be there too. What do you think?"

"Sweet!"

"I'll put these plans into action and we'll see how things are going," Katy said.

Every Saturday, my moms drove me across town to attend Saturday Group. It was fun because I got to play with other kids. The best part came at the end of each day. Before I went home, I'd get to pick a toy from the prize box. I'd get to pick a prize before the other kids if I had a really good day, and followed the rules most of the time. There was even a graduation ceremony when I successfully completed the program. I had my picture taken wearing a long black robe.

I also started going on respite for one weekend a month. That was fun too. Somebody told my folks about a black man who did respite. I started spending my respite weekends with him. He was cool, but there were always a lot of other kids at his house when I was there. I didn't get to spend any time just with him.

A college guy started coming to my house. We played basketball together. For about a month he came every week. We talked a little bit about my Uncle Joey, and how I was still mad at him. The college guy suggested that I write my uncle a letter and tell him about my feelings.

"Go ahead and tell your uncle how angry you are and why," he said.

"I bet you'll feel better once you get some of that off your chest."

I did write my uncle a letter, and then I asked my mom to mail it for me. In my letter I told Uncle Joey about how mean he was to me and to my brother and sister. I told him that it wasn't right for him to treat us that way. I told him that he shouldn't have hurt me. I said that now I was adopted and that he couldn't find me or hurt me ever again. I signed my letter:

Love,
Joshua Radford Carson.

It was fun shooting hoops with the college guy. But after about a month, he graduated and wasn't around anymore.

Jan Crossen

Chapter 11

First Christmas

Jan Crossen

It was my first Christmas with my new family and Mom and I were at the mall. I spotted Santa Clause sitting on a big red chair and pointed him out to my mom.

"Look, Mom," I said. "It's Santa!"

"Do you want to go see him?" she asked.

"Yes, please."

We walked to the end of the line and within a few minutes it was my turn. Santa greeted me with a smile and motioned for me to come closer to him.

"Come on up here," Santa said. "So we can have a little talk."

I moved so that I was standing in front of him.

"I can hear you better, when you're sitting on my lap."

"Go ahead, Josh," Mom said. So I climbed onto his ample thighs.

"So Josh, how's it going for you?" he asked.

"Pretty well."

"We'll I'm glad to hear that. What's been happening since the last time I saw you?"

"I got 'dopted. That's my mom."

I pointed to where my mom was standing. She smiled and waved. There were happy tears spilling out of her eyes.

"Well that's wonderful news, Joshua," Santa said. "I can tell that your mother is happy about having you for a son."

"Yeah," I said. "I have a great family now. I have two moms, five dogs and three cats."

"Well, I'm so happy to hear that. Now tell me what you would like for Christmas this year."

I whispered into his ear. Santa gave me a puzzled look.

"I'm not sure that I heard you correctly. Tell me more about that."

I leaned closer and explained again what I wanted. I turned my head around and showed him my angel kiss.

"Well, Joshua," he said. "That's a very unusual request. I can't promise that you'll get your wish for this Christmas this year. Christmas is less than a week away. But I'll see what I can do for you one of these years, OK?"

"OK," I nodded. "Thank you, Mr. Clause."

"Please, call me Santa, Josh. After all, we've known each other for quite a few years now."

"OK, Santa."

"Shall we take a photo together?" he asked, looking at my mom.

"Yes, please," she said. She still had tears in her eyes. She calls those her 'happy tears.' She explained to me that sometimes her heart gets so happy that tears spill out of her eyes. Happy tears are a good thing

Santa gave me a candy cane and said 'Goodbye.' Another child was waiting to talk with this very important man.

"So what did you tell Santa you wanted for Christmas, Josh?" Mom asked while we waited for our photo to print.

"Is it OK if I tell you some other time?" I asked. "Santa said that I had a very unusual wish. He said that he'd try to get it for me one Christmas, but not this year."

"Hummmmmm, well, all right," Mom said.

Santa's helper handed Mom the photo of Santa and me. She showed it to me.

"Nice photo, Honey."

"Thanks," I said, looking at the picture.

I took her hand and we walked out of the mall and towards our car.

That evening, Momma B, Mom, and I all went out together to pick out our Christmas tree. I knew right away which tree that I wanted. It was extremely round, and was full with branches.

"We'd like that tree," Momma B said to the man who was selling the trees. She pointed to the one that I had selected.

"That one," Mom said. "The tree that's about as round, as it is tall."

Momma B paid for the tree and soon it was in our living room surrounded by boxes of Holiday decorations. My mom found a cassette tape of some old Christmas music and put it on to play.

"When I was growing up," she said, "my family always played this Christmas music when we decorated our trees."

She began singing the songs along with the people on the tape.

"Josh, do you enjoy decorating the Christmas tree?" Momma B asked.

"I don't know," I said. "I've never decorated a tree before."

"Well, we'll have to do something about that now, won't we?" she said, smiling.

I helped my folks untangle the strings of lights and test them before they went on the tree. Then it was time for ornaments.

Josh, we have a special early present for you," Mom said with her hands behind her back.

"What is it?" I asked.

She handed me a small, wrapped box.

"Open it."

Inside was a figurine of a little black boy sitting on the lap of a black Santa.

"It's your very own Christmas ornament," Mom said.

"Is this really for me?"

"You, bet, Sweetheart," Mom said. "And every year you'll get another ornament to add to your collection."

Mom lifted me up so that I could hang my Santa ornament high on the tree.

"Thanks, Moms, I love it."

"You're welcome, Honey," they said together.

"Josh, would you please help me hang these little wooden stars, trees, and the angel ornaments that Grandpa made for us?" Mom asked.

"Sure, but how did he make them?"

"Grandpa makes things out of wood."

"I want to make things out of wood too."

"Well, maybe you and Grandpa can make some things together then?"

"That'd be tight."

"We have a few items that go around the bottom of the tree, Josh," Momma B said, handing me three wooden reindeer.

"Did Grandpa carve these reindeer out of wood too?"

"He sure did," she said.

"Hey look," I said, holding up an animal with a bright red nose. "It's Rudolph!"

Mom found the angel and lifted me up so that I could place her at the top of the tree. Momma B plugged her in and her face began to glow.

"Sweet," I said.

"Yes, it is," Momma B said. "It's nice to have our Guardian Angel keeping watch over us."

"Josh, would you get the little manger out of that box, and put it under the tree?" Mom asked. "This baby doll goes in it."

I found the wooden manger and reached for the doll that Mom was holding.

"Is that Baby Jesus?" I asked.

"Yes."

"But, that's a black baby."

"Well, who said Jesus wasn't black?" Mom asked.

I'd never seen a black baby Jesus before. I cradled the baby doll in my arms and then gently placed the doll in the bed.

"Sleep tight, Baby Jesus," I whispered. "Pleasant dreams."

"Sleep tight is right, Joshie," Mom said. "It's time for bed."

"I need to get a snack for Santa first," I said.

Momma B had made some chocolate chip cookies. I filled a plate and added ice to a glass of milk. I wanted Santa's milk to be nice and cold when he arrived.

I kissed Momma B goodnight and then Mom tucked me into bed. That night I slept very well. I trusted that Santa would find me living with my new family, and that our Guardian Angel would watch over us. I was right about both things. I had a wonderful Christmas with my forever family.

Jan Crossen

Chapter 12

Buffalo Soldiers

"Josh, do you know what tomorrow is?" Mom asked.

"Monday," I said.

"That's right, and it's also Martin Luther King Jr. Day," she said. "Brooke has to work at the animal hospital, but you and I are going to the City Park to take part in the celebration."

"What will we do?" I asked.

"Well, tomorrow is a national holiday to honor Dr. King. There will be a Freedom March, important speakers, African American music, dancing, and food. It'll be fun. Before we go, I want to read the book that I gave you about Dr. King. Would you get it, please?"

"OK."

Mom and I sat on the couch and took turns reading pages from the book about Dr. King.

"I have a dream!" I read the words the way I had heard Dr. King say them on a video that mom bought for me.

"Wow, Josh, you did that very well," Mom said. "It really brings the story to life when you read it that way. I bet you'd be a good actor."

"Thank you."

We finished the story and talked about how important it is for everyone to have equal rights.

"You know, Honey, if Dr. King and his supporters hadn't done the work they did for civil rights, you probably would not be my son."

"What do you mean?"

"People like Dr. King were responsible for African Americans in the United States to finally have the legal rights and opportunities they deserve. Black people were denied these rights in the past.

Dr. King was killed because he fought for equality. He knew that the color of someone's skin didn't matter. He wanted all people to have the same rights and privileges. He led the way to change through peaceful, non-violent methods.

If it weren't for Dr. King and his efforts for civil rights, I never could have adopted you. The law and society would never have allowed it."

"Wow, I never knew that."

The next day Mom and I attended the celebration for Dr. King. It was held outdoors at a park. There were at least a thousand people sitting on benches and blankets. They were listening to the speakers and enjoying the entertainment.

The mayor spoke for a few minutes and welcomed everyone. Some gospel singers came on stage next. They sang some church songs. Then a band came to the stage. They were from a local high school, and they played these shiny bowls called steel drums. After that we heard some Hip-Hop music, and then some tap dancers came onto the stage. I liked the way their feet made snappy sounds to the music. The tapping sounds sounded happy and they made me smile.

A big, bald, black man talked about Dr. King. He recited part of Dr. King's "I Have a Dream" speech. Finally, we watched a dozen black men who were dressed up like pioneer soldiers. They did a marching demonstration. Mom told me they were called the Buffalo Soldiers.

"Josh, do you know who the Buffalo Soldiers were?" Mom asked.

"No, ma'am." I said.

"Well, around the time of the Civil War, the United States government established an all black cavalry."

"What's a cavalry?"

"That's a good question. A cavalry is a military troop that rides horses. They used to travel all over the Southwestern United States on horseback."

"What'd they do?"

"They kept the peace, built roads, protected the mail carriers, and fought in the Indian Wars. And the Buffalo Soldiers were even our nation's first Park Rangers."

"Hummm. Why were they called Buffalo Soldiers?"

"That name was given to them by the Native American Indians from the Cheyenne Nation. The Cheyenne thought the black soldiers were fierce fighters. And when the hair of the black men grew long, it reminded the Natives of the hide on a buffalo. The words 'Buffalo Soldier' mean 'Wild Buffalo' in the Cheyenne language. It was a term of respect."

"That's tight."

"Yes it is, Josh, yes it is."

Jan Crossen

Chapter 13

Roller Ranch

The next fall, I was in the fourth grade at Lineweaver Elementary School. My school was having a skating party as a way to raise money.

"Mom, may I please go to our school skating party?" I asked. "It's at Roller Ranch and it sounds like fun. I really want to go."

"Do you know how to skate, Honey?" Mom asked.

"Not really. But I can learn," I said. "Pretty please?"

Mom laughed and agreed to take me to Roller Ranch the next night.

I could hardly wait to get in the door.

Popular music blasted from the DJ stand. A lot of kids from my school were already on the floor.

"You'll need some rental skates," Mom said leading the way to the rental booth. "Size 3, please," she said to the teenage boy working there.

I lifted the heavy boots from the counter and we headed for the benches. Mom helped me lace the skates so that they were tight. Hoping to quickly learn how to skate, I studied the other kids as they skated past.

"Wish me luck," I said, holding onto the wall. I inched my way onto the rink.

"Good luck and have fun," Mom said.

She found a seat and watched the skaters. I shuffled slowly around the floor. Some kids blew past me. Their skates made a roar as they pounded the wooden floor. A few of the kids could skate forwards and backwards. The older kids even danced on their skates to the music. They were really good!

"OK," the disc jockey said from atop his perch. "It's time for some skating games."

The DJ's booth was at least four feet above the crowd. He had a great view of everything that was happening on the floor of the rink.

I left the rink and stood on the sidelines. That night I just watched the games and races. I knew there was no way that I could compete at roller-skating. But I had fun watching and being part of the school event.

The next day at breakfast Mom asked me a question. "Josh, are you interested in taking skating lessons? They offer them at Roller Ranch and there is a new class starting this Saturday morning."

"That would be awesome," I said. "Thanks, Mom!"

Saturday morning I was up early. I was eager for my first skating lesson.

There were eight kids in my class. My teacher was an older woman who was very patient. She'd teach us something as a group. Then she'd work with each of us by ourselves.

Going to Roller Ranch became a regular part of my weekly schedule. I would rent my skates and carefully go onto the floor. Mom always waited during my lesson. Then she'd let me skate for a while when the rink opened to the public.

Skating lessons lasted for twelve weeks. By the end I was skating well. I could skate forwards and backwards, and even do a crossover step.

My confidence grew as my skills improved.

Chapter 14

On Your Mark...

Jan Crossen

In the spring my school sponsored another skate party and this time I was ready. It turned out the event was scheduled on the same day as my tenth birthday.

That night my folks took me to Roller Ranch. I got my skates from the rental stand and laced them up. Stepping confidently onto the floor, I joined the other kids. I skated in time with the music, and bobbed up and down. I turned around and skated backwards. I was awesome, and it was a blast!

"OK, kids," the DJ said. "It's time for the races."

The races were divided by age and sex. Because it was my birthday, I would compete against the older kids. Those were the kids who were between 10 and 12 years old.

First the younger girls raced, and then came the younger boys. Next it was the older girls' turn to test their speed on skates. Finally, they called my age group. I joined the older boys at the start line.

All of them were taller and bigger than I was. That wasn't going to scare me. Finding my spot near the front of the pack, I was ready to race.

"On your mark, get set, GO!" the DJ shouted.

I took off, but was jammed up in the middle of the group. I tried to move closer to the inside of the track. I wanted some space to really pump my arms and build up some speed. A hole opened up and I went for it.

'Skate, skate, skate, skate.' I thought to myself.

We were halfway around the rink, and I was one of six guys in the lead.

"Faster, faster," I told myself. "Go, go, go, go!"

I pushed harder moving my legs as quickly as they would go. One boy caught his skate on something. He slipped and fell taking two other skaters with him. I wobbled as I dodged the fallen bodies all around me. I managed to stay on my feet. Now there were only three of us.

"Go Josh, Go!" My parents clapped and cheered for me.

There was a lot of noise as the kids screamed and yelled for their friends.

Then… there was total silence. Everything began to move in slow motion. I looked over my right shoulder. A big kid, with long brown hair, moved up next to me. He looked at me, and our eyes locked in a serious challenge. He moved his left arm across his chest. I thought he was about to throw an elbow in my direction.

Using a crossover step I avoided his jab, and moved out in front. I grunted, leaned forward, and crossed the finish line first. I HAD WON!

Throwing my arms up into the air, I screamed with delight. "WWWWOOOOOOOOOO HOOOOOOOOOOOOOOOOOO!" I yelled. "I did it! I won!"

It felt so good! I skated quickly over to my parents who were smiling and clapping for me.

"I've never won a race before in my life!" I shouted to them.

Everybody congratulated me. Kids gave me high fives and slapped me on the back. My folks were excited and hugged me.

"It's time to award the prizes to our winners," the DJ said. "Would the winner from each race please come to the DJ stand to get your trophy?"

I eagerly joined the other winners at the front of the DJ box. Each one of us received a small gold trophy. There was a figurine of a roller skater on top.

Looking closely at the trophy made me smile even more. The skater was posed raising his arms victoriously over his head. It was the same thing that I did after winning the race. Turning ten years old was an awesome birthday, and one that I'll never forget.

Chapter 15

Karate Kid

"Mom, I want to take karate lessons," I said one day in early September. "They offer them at the YMCA. It'd be really cool if I could learn how to do that."

I pictured myself being Daniel LaRusso in the "Karate Kid" movies. "Wax on, wax off, paint the fence," I thought to myself. I dreamed of doing the one-legged crane kick and winning the girl and the tournament at the same time.

My parents decided that taking skating lessons had helped my self-esteem, so they agreed to give me karate lessons.

"OK," Mom said, "you can give karate a try. We'll need to find you a gui to wear."

"What's a gui?" I asked.

"A gui is the karate uniform," Momma B said. "It's those white baggy pants with the big shirt that you tie with a cloth belt. Everyone in your class will wear one."

My parents bought me a brand new gui, and I was ready for my first class. My folks dropped me off, at the karate room, and then went to workout in the fitness room at the YMCA. An hour and a half later they picked me up at my classroom door.

"So how did it go, Josh?" Mom asked.

"Great," I said.

"Do you like your teacher?" Momma B asked.

"You mean sensei," I said. "That means teacher."

Just then my sensei walked out into the hall. He waved to us and we waved back.

"Wow," Momma B said. "He's wearing a Black Belt."

"What does that mean?" I asked.

"It means you'd better pay attention in class because he's really good at karate," she teased me.

"I see that most of the kids in your class have white belts like you do," Mom said. "But look at those kids. That boy and girl are wearing different colored belts. The boy has on a yellow belt and the girl's belt is green."

"That's because they're assistants to Sensei," I said. "They aren't beginners like the rest of us. You can tell that they've taken karate before.

Sensei said the boy has already earned the first level belt with color, and the girl has earned her second level belt."

"Cool," Mom said.

"Way cool," said Momma B.

"So what'd you learn today?" Mom asked.

"We learned to bow," I said.

"Why do you bow?" Momma B asked.

101

"We bow to Sensei to show respect. We bowed before class starts, and to each opponent, and then we bowed to Sensei again at the end of the lesson."

"That's impressive," Momma B said.

"Sensei wants us to do ten push-ups at the beginning of every class. That was too easy for me so I did twenty instead. See my muscles?" I flexed my right arm and then my left.

"Those are some nice looking biceps, Josh," Mom said.

"Thanks," I said, and then kissed each one. I loved looking at my developing muscles.

"Tonight we learned how to fall and hit the ground without getting hurt. We did a lot of tumble rolls and slapped our hands down hard on the mat. I even learned some moves to take my opponent down."

"It sounds as though you had a good workout tonight."

"Yes, ma'am, and now I'm starving!"

My folks laughed.

Karate lessons lasted for three months.

"Class, this week we have our final two practices before the competition," Sensei said. "The competition is on Saturday, starting at 9:00 a.m."

"What do we do, how does this work?" another student asked.

"Each of you has been learning a certain routine," Sensei said. "Now it is time for you to perform it in front of the judges. I'll be a judge and so will three other master teachers. Any other questions?"

No one spoke or raised a hand. We sat on the floor shaking our heads.

All week long I practiced my routine. I'd put on my gui and go into the backyard to practice.

Mom got me up early on Saturday morning so that I could have a good breakfast before the competition. I put on my gui and was ready.

My parents were very nervous and excited for me. They found two seats in the front row so that they could take a lot of pictures of me when I did my routine.

"Good luck, Josh!" they said when Sensei called my name.

I walked to the center of the floor, looked at Sensei and bowed.

"Begin," he said. He looked very serious.

I focused my mind on the routine and did my moves with power and confidence. I finished and bowed at Sensei. He dismissed me from the floor. My folks cheered, clapped, and whistled. I smiled with embarrassment.

At the end of the day, Sensei gave out awards. "Joshua Carson," he said.

I walked to where he was standing and bowed. He bowed and handed me a Certificate of Achievement. I was proud of myself and of my success in karate. Momma B framed my karate certificate and hung it on my bedroom wall.

Driving home that afternoon I told my folks, "Thank you for giving me karate lessons. I liked karate, but don't want to do that anymore."

My parents sighed and then smiled shaking their heads.

Chapter 16

Miss Bianca

"I want to tap dance," I said.

"I take it you liked the movie 'Tap' that we watched the other night?" Momma B said.

A black actor named Gregory Hines was a tap dancer in the movie. He was great.

"Yeah, he was the bomb!" I said.

My folks decided that tap dancing would be another good way to build my confidence. They agreed to look for a teacher. A few days later mom told me the good news.

"Josh, I've located the African American woman whose dance class performed at the Martin Luther King Jr. celebration. She teaches dance and has a new tap class starting this coming Saturday morning," Mom said. "Do you still want to dance?"

"Yes, ma'am, thank you." I said with a smile. "I'll need tap shoes."

"You're right. We'll see about getting some today," Momma B said.

We found a store that sold kid's tap shoes. They were beautiful, black, patent leather. I loved the way they smelled, and the clicking sounds they made when I tried them on in the store.

"Josh, these are very expensive shoes. If we're going to spend this kind of money, I need you to tell me that you aren't going to quit after a month or two," Mom said.

"I won't quit, I really want to dance." I promised.

We bought the shoes and I couldn't wait to try them out. As soon as we returned home, I grabbed my boom box and new tap shoes and ran to the garage. I started dancing, just like Gregory Hines, all over the cement floor.

On Saturday morning Mom and I headed to Miss Bianca's class together. Her studio was on the second floor of an old building on the other side of town.

There were a dozen other black kids in my class. It was nice for me to be around other black people. My world was filled with white faces and this was a nice change.

An attractive black woman entered the room. She was 5'6" tall, thin, and had strong arms and legs. Her hair was long and wiry. She wore it on top of her head, held back with a yellow elastic band. She greeted us with a warm smile.

"Welcome everyone," she said, "My name is Bianca Willis. You may call me Miss Bianca. I've been giving dance lessons in this town for thirty years. I recognize some of your parents as former students of mine. I'm looking forward to dancing with each of you."

I could tell that Miss Bianca was a respected teacher.

"Do you all know who started tap dance?" she asked the class.

No one had an answer.

"Well, tap dance was started by African slaves a long time ago. You're going to learn a dance that was started by your ancestors. What do you think of that?"

"Tight," I answered.

"And who are you, young man?" she asked me.

"I'm Joshua Carson, ma'am. That's my mom over there," I said, pointing to where my mother was sitting. Mom waved at the introduction.

"It's nice to meet you, Joshua. Who else do we have in this class?"

Miss Bianca listened while each student said his or her name.

"OK, let's dance!" She walked over to the tape player and started the music.

Miss Bianca clapped to the beat and then started doing some dance moves. We followed her lead. The rhythm of the metal taps sounded against the wooden floor.

'Tap, tap, clap, clap, tap, tap, clap, clap.'

"That's called a shuffle ball change," Miss Bianca said.

For an hour and a half I worked hard, following her example and learning my tap steps. When class was over and we got home, I showed Momma B what I had learned in class.

"That's very impressive, Josh. You've got great sense of rhythm. You must get that from your mom," she said with a smile.

I nodded in agreement.

The next week Miss Bianca told us that she had an announcement to make.

"We'll be learning a routine and giving a performance in a couple of months. Your parents, family, and friends will be invited to be in the audience. Let's really focus and see what we can accomplish today."

Every night I practiced on the cement floor of our garage at home.

Before I knew, it was time for our show. My folks dropped me at the stage door and took a front row seat. They planned to video tape my performance.

Several other acts went on before it was time for our class of beginners. Finally, it was our turn.

"Clap-clap; clap-clap; clap-clap, clap-clap," the metal on the bottom of our shoes announced our arrival on stage. We hurried into position, and smiled proudly as we waited for our music to begin.

I danced my very best and had a great time! Our time on stage went by too quickly. It was hard to believe the music had stopped and we needed to leave the floor.

The audience erupted with applause as we left the stage. I smiled and threw kisses to them. I tossed a kiss first with one hand, then with the other hand, and finally with both hands.

"Come on, Josh, get off the stage," a kid behind me said.

It was great being on stage and being the center of attention. I waved to my folks and stepped down from the platform.

My parents had spent a lot of money on my tap shoes and dance lessons. Gas was expensive and mom had driven me across town every weekend for my

Jan Crossen

classes. I had my moment in the spotlight. I wasn't sure how to tell them that I no longer wanted to continue with my tap dance lessons.

Chapter 17

Piano Guy

Momma B played piano when she was a young girl. Her piano sat in the living room of our home. Sometimes I'd ask her if I could play it, even though I didn't know how. Most of the time she said, "Yes."

"Moms, I want to take piano lessons," I said one Sunday evening.

"Someone told me that playing a musical instrument helps kids do better in math," Mom said to her partner. "What do you think?"

"Well, Josh doesn't abuse my piano," Momma B said. "When he sits down to play, he usually comes up with pleasant sounds. Josh, you may practice on my piano as long as you continue to be respectful of it."

Mom found a piano teacher, Judy Kane, who was taking new students. She was a petite, white woman who taught kids how to play the piano. For a whole year I went to her house once a week for my lessons.

"We have two piano recitals each year," Mrs. Kane told Mom and me. "Our first one is scheduled in three months.

"What's a recital?" I asked.

"A recital is when you play the piano for an audience," said Mrs. Kane. "When my students have a recital, the audience is usually just friends and family who come to hear them play."

"OK," I said.

"For our recitals, we play on a big, beautiful, black, Grand piano. It belongs to the parents of one of my students. They graciously allow us to use it and their home for our recitals."

"Wow, I get to play on a real Grand piano? Sweet!" I said.

"Well, you need to practice every day and memorize your music first," said Mrs. Kane. "You'll play one number by yourself. Then you and I will play a duet together. How does that sound?"

"Great!"

"We have a lot of work to do to prepare for it," she said. "Let's get busy."

I practiced a lot so that I could memorize my musical pieces for the recital. My teacher expected us to perform without looking at the music, but it was always on the piano just in case we forgot.

Some days when I was supposed to be practicing I'd just sit at the piano and make up my own creations. I really like playing music that I create much more than I like playing music that somebody else has written.

"Josh, that was very nice," Mom said from the kitchen. "But it doesn't sound like either of the songs you're playing in the recital."

"I made it up," I said.

113

"Maybe you need to rehearse your recital songs first, and when you're finished practicing you can spend some time creating your own music."

"OK," I said.

On the day of the recital I wore a nice shirt and my dress slacks. Our family friend, Jillian Johnson, went with my parents to see and hear me play. Jillian had attended my Naming Ceremony when I was first adopted. She was a good friend of our family.

"Are you nervous, Josh?" Jillian asked.

"No," I said shaking my head. "I'm ready."

"Break-a-leg," she said. "That's what you say to an actor before he goes on stage. I'm not sure what you're supposed to say to a musician to wish him good luck."

She smiled and gave me a hug. My moms hugged me too, and then I walked over to sit with the rest of the kids.

Mrs. Kane had about six other kids play before she called my name. I walked to the front of the group.

"Hello, my name is Joshua Radford Carson, and it's my pleasure to play for you. I hope you enjoy my music."

I sat down and began to play. I didn't even think about the audience. I was really into my music. I finished the song and the people clapped. My teacher walked over to the piano. I stood up and announced that we would now play a duet. We sounded good together and it was fun.

After my second recital, I told my moms that I didn't want to take piano lessons anymore. I still liked the piano, but I was tired of being told how to play other people's music. For a while, I just wanted to make my own music.

That Christmas my parents surprised me with an electric keyboard. It was tight! It had 76 keys and I could add in 100 different background instruments. It came with a stand and a stool. I spent hours in my bedroom with my keyboard making up beats.

Jan Crossen

Chapter 18

Hoops

"Mom, I want to play basketball," I said.

"OK, let me finish tossing the laundry in the machine and then I'll join you in the driveway," Mom said.

For my tenth birthday my folks had given me a new basketball and hoop. They asked a neighbor to install a backboard above the garage, so our driveway became my court.

Mom used to be the head coach for high school girls' basketball team, and an assistant coach for a college team. She taught me some ball handling skills and how to shoot and dribble. I was a better offensive player than a defensive one. I spent hours outside in the driveway perfecting my long shot.

"That's not what I mean," I said. "I want to do more than just shoot. I need to play on a team. Can you please find me a basketball team?"

"The City Recreation Department has youth basketball leagues," Mom said. "We'll find out when their leagues start."

Two weeks later I was registered for the upcoming season. We had practice or games every Tuesday and Friday evening.

"Momma B, I'm having trouble breathing," I said. "Every time that I run down the floor, I start wheezing."

"You may have exercise-induced asthma," Momma B said.

"Coach has to take me out of every game so that I can catch my breath. I miss too much of the action just sitting on the sidelines!"

Mom took me to the doctor who said that I had a breathing problem, which was caused by hard running.

"Joshua has asthma brought on by exercise," he said. "Let's try using this inhaler and see if it helps when he's playing sports. Take two puffs a few minutes before you play. And let me know if it doesn't help."

The next day at practice I used the inhaler. My breathing was a lot better and I was able to stay in the game.

"Josh would you like to go to a summer basketball camp?" Mom asked. "It's Lute Olson's camp. He's the coach of the men's basketball team at the University of Arizona."

"I know who he is, Mom," I said. "And, yes, I'd love to go!"

Every day, for a week, Mom drove me to McKale Center on the University of Arizona campus. There must have been 200 kids there.

Mom always asked me questions when she picked me up at the end of each day.

"How was camp, Honey?" Mom asked.

"Good," I said, and stared out the window.

Mom waited a few seconds and then began asking more questions.

"Tell me about your day, Josh."

"I don't know what to say."

"Well, what did you learn?"

"I don't know."

"What did you do?"

"We played basketball."

"I know that, Josh. Can you tell me anything specific that you did?"

"I don't remember.

"Josh, you just left the gym after spending the entire day there. How can you not remember what you just did?"

"I don't know."

"Hummmmm. Did you have any trouble with your breathing?"

"No."

"Did you need your inhaler?"

"Yes, ma'am."

"Good job. Do you still have it with you?"

"I don't know."

"Would you please look for it in your gym bag?"

I searched by backpack. "It's not here. It must be in the gym someplace."

"Oh, Josh. Let's go see if we can find it now. If we wait until tomorrow, you may never see it again."

Mom parked the car and we returned to the gym floor. Mom talked with one of the coaches and explained our problem. He asked some other kids to help us look for my inhaler. We looked all over the gym, the locker room, and where we ate lunch. Finally, a tall kid with short red hair walked up to us. He handed me my inhaler.

"I found this on the floor of the boy's restroom," he said.

"Thank you so much!" Mom said.

"Thanks, man," I said.

"No problem," he said, and walked away.

"Honey, you need to keep better track of your things. It could be dangerous for you if you needed your inhaler, but couldn't find it."

"O.K."

Mom and I returned to our car and headed home.

"Did you see Coach Olson today?"

"Yes, I even had my picture taken with him. He's going to autograph it for me."

"Wow, that'll be nice to have."

At the end of the week the coaches handed out the photographs. Momma B framed mine and hung it on my bedroom wall.

"Josh, this is a nice photo of you and Coach Olson," Mom said. "He's a basketball legend, Honey. He's one of the best."

"Sweet," I said admiring the newest picture on my wall.

"Very sweet," Mom said smiling.

Photo used with permission from Coach Lute Olson and
Chic Haase Photography, Inc., Tucson, AZ.

Chapter 19

Whispering Hope Ranch

My parents discovered a wonderful place called Whispering Hope Ranch. It's way out in the country near Payson, Arizona. One weekend, my folks took me there for a visit. It was a long ride but definitely worth it.

The Ranch is about 25 miles outside of Payson. We drove through the beautiful Ponderosa Pine trees. Their tree trunks smelled like vanilla, and I thought that was cool. This is elk country so we kept our eyes open for them as we drove along the road.

My mom is an excellent critter spotter. Grandpa taught her how, and she was teaching me. We knew that if there were any elk or deer around, Mom would point them out for us.

There is an electric gate at the entrance to the Ranch. Momma B pushed the button and the gate slowly swung open. The car made a crunching sound as we drove the long gravel driveway to the parking area.

"Hi, and welcome to Whispering Hope Ranch," a pretty, dark haired woman said, as she stepped off the porch to meet us. "I'm Diane Reid, the founder of the Ranch."

My folks shook her hand and introduced each of us. A beautiful, brown tabby cat ran towards us and rubbed against my leg.

"That's Strawberry," Diane said. "She lives here along with a dozen other cats."

"I love cats," I said. "She's beautiful."

"We noticed the horses along the driveway, what other animals do you have here?" Momma B asked.

"The Ranch is home to over one hundred animals," Diane said. "There are horses, cows, goats, burros, pigs, emus, and llamas. We also have peacocks, ducks, dogs, cats, sheep, deer, and bunnies here."

"Why are there so many animals?" I asked.

"Well, because the Ranch is a safe place for animals that have been abused or neglected, or for those that have a physical deformity," Diane said. "These animals never did any thing to hurt anyone, but they've been hurt by people. Now they're learning to trust again, and are helping people feel better and enjoy life."

"May we take a look around?" I asked.

"Of course," Diane said. "Let me get a golf cart and I'll take you on a tour of the ranch myself. With the cart, we can ride in style."

We loaded into the cart and Diane began telling us about the animals. She told us the name and story of every animal that we saw.

"People visit the Ranch to see and interact with the animals," Diane said. "Being with the animals helps them feel better and enjoy themselves."

"Can anybody come to the Ranch?" Mom asked.

Jan Crossen

"Yes, everyone is welcome, but we are especially helpful for someone who is grieving, going through a difficult time, or has an illness like diabetes, autism, Downs Syndrome, or cancer."

We came to a fenced pasture. It was the home to four llamas. Getting out of the car Diane called, "Tony, Tony, come here Sweetheart, come and meet Josh and his moms."

All four of the llamas walked over to the fence.

"This handsome guy is Tony Llama," Diane said. "He really likes to give kisses. Go stand by him, Joshua, and he'll give you a kiss."

I walked to the fence and looked at the large beast. He leaned his face over the wooden bar and tickled my cheek with a kiss.

"Oh, my goodness!" I said rubbing my cheek. "That's funny!"

I touched my cheek to show him that I wanted another kiss, which he quickly gave me.

"Is that a donkey?" I asked pointing into the next pasture area.

"Actually," Diane said, "Those are miniature burros. That's 'Hugs' closest to us. The darker one is named 'Cuddles.'"

Diane opened their gate and the two animals came out of their pen. I threw my arm around 'Hugs' and mom took my picture.

We continued our tour and came to some Indian teepees.

"What are the teepees for?" I asked Diane.

"We use those for sleeping when the Native American kids come for the Diabetes Camp," she said.

"This place is amazing," Momma B said. "Who's your veterinarian?"

Diane talked with my folks about the health care for the animals while I went off into the woods exploring by myself.

"We'd like to do something for the Ranch," Momma B said. "Would it help if we brought our hospital staff up here and examined and vaccinated the dogs, cats, and horses? We would donate our services and the vaccine."

"That would be wonderful!" Diane said.

Momma B made arrangements for us to do just that. In the fall, we had our first Staff Retreat at Whispering Hope Ranch. It was snowing when we arrived on a Saturday afternoon. I had a blast playing in the snow.

It was the mating season for the elk. At dusk we took at ride in the car and saw at least a dozen of the large animals. They're really big, and they came so close to our car. That evening we could hear the elk bugling. They were trying to attract the females. It was noisy and made me laugh.

The next day Momma B examined each dog, cat, and horse, and then she vaccinated each one. I had a great time helping take care of the animals.

On Sunday, we played in the snow. Instead of making a snow man, we made a snow-cat. It was time to return to Tucson, and I could hardly wait for our next trip to Whispering Hope Ranch.

Chapter 20

Do You Believe in Magic?

When I was ten years old, my folks had taken me to Las Vegas, Nevada.

It was awesome! We got tickets to see Lance Armstrong, a professional magician, do his show. I was really into magic, and sat on the edge of my seat for the entire performance. That's when I knew that I wanted to do magic too.

There was a magic shop in Las Vegas and my folks bought me a card trick. I studied and practiced that trick until I could do it perfectly. I asked everybody I knew if they wanted to see it.

My folks found a magician who also lived in Tucson. His name was George Cotton. He and his wife, Christy, did a magic show at a local dinner theatre. They were also barbers so I started having George cut my hair. I'd ask mom for a haircut even when I didn't need one, just so I could spend time with George.

"You like magic, huh?" George said to me on our first meeting.

"Yes, sir, I do!" I answered with a big grin.

George took a quarter out of his pocket and bit it in half. He showed it to me and I could see that half of it was gone. Then he spit on the half quarter that was in his hand. Immediately, the other half of the coin appeared and it was whole again.

"Tight!" I said.

"Do you know any magic, Joshua?" he asked.

"I sure do."

"OK, show me."

I did the one and only card trick that I knew.

"That's pretty good, Joshua," he said. "How would you like to work with me at my magic show on Saturday night?"

"Oh my gosh, yes!"

"Great, I have a couple of other young boys who work with me, too," George said. "You'll do what we call close-up magic."

"What's that?"

"It's magic that you perform with your audience sitting at a table right in front of you."

"Sweet."

"You do your magic before my magic show starts, and while the people are waiting to be served their dinner. You walk up to the table and say, 'My name is Joshua. May I please do some magic for you?' If they say 'Yes,' then you do the exact same card trick for them, that you just did for me. Can you do that?"

"Sure!"

"Good, when the trick is over, you bow and say, 'Thank you.' Then you move on to another table."

"That sounds great."

"OK, but I have a couple of rules."

I listened carefully to what George was about to say.

"You need to practice your magic over and over again, so that it's perfect."

"OK."

"Do you have a pair of dress slacks, a white long sleeved shirt and a tie?" He looked at my mom who nodded her head.

"He has a black suit if you'd like him to wear that," Mom said.

"Perfect," George said. "And you've got to have clean, short fingernails. A magician always has clean hands and well manicured nails."

We left the barbershop and I went home to practice my magic. George told my mom where I needed to be for the performance on Saturday night, and at what time.

Momma B made an appointment for me to have a professional manicure so that my nails would be perfect for my performance. Mom made reservations for Momma B and her to have dinner and see the magic show that night.

I was excited about doing up-close magic. It was fun working with George and his wife, Christy. It was especially fun when some of the people tipped me after I had completed my magic. By the end of the night I had made $15.00 in tips!

Mom bought me books about magic. I even got a Lance Armstrong video about how to do magic. Tucson has a magic store, and I asked for magic tricks for my birthday. I spent my birthday money buying new tricks, too. I practiced a lot, and got pretty good.
For my birthday, my grandpa made me a magician's table. I loved performing for my grandparents.

"How does he do that?" Grandma always used to say as she clapped for me.

"Do that again, Joshua," Grandpa would say, shaking his head in amazement. "Do it slower next time."

Jan Crossen

"Sorry, Grandpa," I'd say. "But a magician only does each trick one time, and a magician never reveals his secrets."

My parent's had a good friend named Jean Murphy. Sometimes I would be invited to go to lunch with Jean and my folks. One day she told me that she had just returned from a trip to Las Vega, Nevada. She had bought something for me while she was there. Jean handed me a large, square, box that I quickly opened. Inside was a beautiful gold magician's hat.

"Josh, I saw that top hat, with these flashy gold sequins on it, and I just knew that you should have it," Jean said. "I thought you could use it for your magic."

"Wow!" I said admiring my gift. I quickly gave her a thank you hug and kiss on the cheek. "This is awesome! Thank you!"

Jean knew that I was dreaming of a career as a famous magician who performed in Las Vegas. Her gift was perfect for me.

Chapter 21

Martin Luther King III

The next summer my mom got a phone call from Diane Reid at Whispering Hope Ranch. She invited my family to go there for a weekend. She said that she wanted us to meet Martin Luther King, III. He's the son of the famous civil rights leader, Dr. Martin Luther King, Jr.

At the time, Mr. King had a cable television program called, 'Wisdom of Dreams.' He was doing a story about Whispering Hope Ranch.

It was Diane's dream to have a safe place where abandoned, abused, and neglected animals could live. It would also be a place where people could go. They could relax and spend time with the animals. Diane says that a special kind of magic happens between people and the animals at the ranch. The animals help the people heal.

My parents took me to the Ranch and I got to meet Mr. King. Diane introduced my parents and me to him. He was a really nice guy and I liked spending time with him.

"Mr. King, would you please autograph these two books that I brought with me? They're about your dad," I said to him.

"It would be my pleasure, Joshua," he said. And then he signed my books.

"Thank you, Mr. King," my mom said. "Those are very special books, and we'll keep them forever."

"Please, call me Martin," he said.

Mr. King asked my moms how we met and how we became a family. Mom told him about me being a miracle baby that was born two months early. She told him about how I survived a coma, and about my near drowning.

"You're one lucky guy, Joshua," he said. "You remind me of a lucky cat."

"My nickname is 'Cat,'" I said.

"Well it certainly seems to fit you," Mr. King said.

I had my picture taken with Mr. King and then he asked my mom a question.

"I do a television program called 'Wisdom of Dreams.' I'd like to interview you and Joshua about your adoption," he said. "And I'd like to talk about what Whispering Hope Ranch means to you. We'd include it in our segment about the Ranch. What do you say?"

"Josh would you like Mr. King to interview us?" Mom said.

"Sure," I said.

So Mr. King, Mom, and I all sat down inside one of the teepees. The cameraman started shooting, and Mr. King asked questions.

"Joshua, why do you like coming to the Ranch?" he asked me.

"I love the freedom that I have here," I said. "I get to explore all over and play with the animals. I help feed and water them, and once I got to drive the golf cart."

"Do you have a favorite animal at the Ranch?" Mr. King asked.

"Well, yes, I have two favorites," I said, "Strawberry Cream Pie; she's a great cat, and Tony Llama, because he gives kisses."

"Ms. Carson, why do you like to bring your son to Whispering Hope Ranch?"

"It's such a peaceful place, with so many wonderful animals," Mom said. "Josh has a great time and it's so good for his self-esteem."

"How so?"

"The Ranch is a safe place, the animals are gentle, and the staff and volunteers are welcoming. They make everyone feel important," Mom answered. "Josh hangs with the guys, does farm chores, and interacts with the animals and people. It's a great experience for him and for all of us."

Mom and Mr. King talked about my mother's dream of adopting a son. Mom said that the work done by Mr. King's father helped to make that dream come true.

At the end of the filming, I walked out of our teepee, and over to the outside of another one. With red paint I wrote, 'Wisdom of Dreams.' My painting has been on that teepee ever since.

The story about Whispering Hope Ranch was on TV a few months later, and my story was part of it.

Diane sent my family a copy of the video, so we can watch it again any time that we like.

I never thought that I'd get to meet somebody as important at Martin Luther King, III. It was an amazing day, and one that I won't forget.

When we shook hands and said goodbye Mr. King handed me his business card and said, "If I can ever do anything for you, Josh, here is where you can find me. I'd love to help you in any way that I can."

"Sweet," I said. "Thank you, Sir."

We said goodbye to Diane, the staff, and volunteers who work at the Ranch, and headed back to Tucson.

Jan Crossen

Chapter 22

Heritage Camp

When I was thirteen, my family drove to Denver, Colorado so that I could go to the African American Cultural Heritage Camp. That's a weekend camp for black or biracial kids who've been adopted by parents who aren't black. 'Biracial' means that a person has parents who are from two different races. The Heritage Camp showed me that I wasn't the only kid who had white parents.

"Josh, there will be African American kids at this camp, and also some kids who were adopted from Africa," Mom said.

"And there are camps all summer long," said Momma B. "They have camps for kids who are adopted from Korea, China, Vietnam, India, Russia, and probably other countries too."

"Sweet," I said.

Heritage camp was a blast. The parents went to meetings while the kids did cool things. We beat on drums from Africa, listened to Rap music and got down with some hip-hop dancing. We also learned about some famous black people.

Each kid was given the name of an important black person. We found out about our person and then gave a performance where we pretended to be that person. The adults and other campers tried to guess who we were supposed to be from the hints that we gave them.

I was Louis Armstrong. He was a famous jazz trumpet player. His nickname was 'Satchmo,' and he carried a white handkerchief with him to wipe the sweat from his face.

When it was my turn, I jumped on the stage carrying a white Kleenex. I turned to the crowd with a big smile. I used a gravelly voice and said, "Hey, all you cats, welcome to my gig. Ha, ha, ha. I was born in New Orleans, Louisiana back in 1901. My sweet Grandmother raised me 'til I was 12 years old. As a kid, I learned to play the trumpet, and later I started something called 'scat' singing. Some famous singers like Billie Holiday and Ella Fitzgerald followed this style. One of my hit recordings was 'Hello Dolly.' Can you guess who I am?"

Then I dabbed my forehead and pretended to play the trumpet. The grown-ups called out, "Satchmo, Louie Armstrong." It was fun.

One day we had a picnic in the park. We ate fried chicken and played games. It was great!

"Parents, campers, may I have your attention please?" the camp director said.

We all stopped what we were doing and came over to where she was standing so that we could hear what she was about to say.

"Tomorrow night is our last night," she said.

Everyone said, "Booooooooooooooooooooooo."

"So we have a special party planned that should be a lot of fun."

The 'boos' turned into cheers.

"Yeahhhhhhhhhhhhhhhhhhhhhhhhhhhhhhhhhhh."

"We're having a Roaring Twenties party. The girls will come as flappers, those were flashy dancers from a long time ago, and the boys will be the handsome gentlemen."

The next evening everyone got dressed up. The girls wore short dresses and long beads. I put on my black suit, a white shirt, white socks, and black tie. I wore my shiny, black, patent leather dress shoes. I must admit that I looked good.

The party room was decorated with a lot of little, round tables that were covered with sheets. It was supposed to look like a nightclub.

We had a DJ who played a lot of music from the 1920's. After a while, I asked him to play some music so that we could dance. I asked for something by Michael Jackson. The DJ played 'Billy Jean, Thriller, and Beat It' for me.

"Come on, Cat, do Michael Jackson for us," the kids said at the party. "Michael, Michael, Michael, Michael," they chanted.

It didn't take much coaxing for me to jump onto the stage. I took off my tie and jacket and unbuttoned several buttons of my shirt. I pulled a sparkling silver glove out of my front pocket and put it on my right hand.

The sounds of "Beat It" pulsed, and I started my moves. I did a head nod, then jerked and twitched. I did the Moon Walk, spun around, and kicked. By now my shirt was partly off my shoulders. I grabbed my crotch then went up on my toes. The crowd went wild cheering for me and I beamed with pride. It was tight, and definitely my favorite part of camp!

Jan Crossen

Chapter 23

A Christmas Wish

It was fall and Halloween was fast approaching. Already, I was dreaming about Christmas.

"Moms, I want something very special for Christmas this year," I said to my parents one Saturday morning in mid-October.

"What's that, Cat-Honey?" Mom asked.

"I'd like my angel kiss to disappear," I said. "I want to look normal. I'm tired of people asking me about it and making fun of me."

My folks looked at each other, and then Mom said, "We'll see what we can do about that, Josh."

My mom made an appointment for me to meet with a plastic surgeon.

He examined my scar and then said, "I can't make your angel kiss disappear completely, Joshua, but I can make it a lot smaller. After surgery, it'll look like a thin line. Will that work for you?"

"Yes, sir, thank you!" I told him.

My surgery was scheduled for the Thursday before we started our Christmas break from school. My folks and I got up from bed while it was still dark outside. We drove to the hospital on the far northwest part of town.

"Good morning," Mom said to the woman behind the hospital desk. "This is my son, Joshua Carson. He's here for surgery this morning."

The lady had mom sign a bunch of papers and then my parents and I were taken to a room where I changed into a stupid looking hospital gown. Dr. Gibbs, my surgeon, and another doctor came by to see me. They explained what they were going to do to fix my head, and asked me if I were ready.

"Yes, sir, I'm definitely ready," I said.

My mom kissed my angel spot and then she kissed my cheek.

"See you in a little while, Honey. I love you," she said.

Momma B kissed my forehead and said, "See you later, alligator."

"After while, crocodile," I said back.

Mom and I signed, "I love you" in sign language, and then we touched fingers. Mom blew me a kiss, which I pretended to catch, and I blew one back to her. She caught it, and we each touched our "kiss" to our cheeks at the same time. My parents left the room.

"I'm going to put this mask over your nose and mouth, Joshua," one of the doctors said to me. "You'll start to smell the gas which will help you go to sleep. You won't feel a thing during your surgery. I promise. OK?"

"OK."

He placed the mask over my face.

"I want you to count out loud to me. Count backwards from 10 to 1, Josh, and just breathe normally."

I began to count for him. I could hear my voice. "Ten, nine, eight, sev…" That was the last thing I remember.

"Joshua, wake up. It's all over and it's time for you to wake up now," a nurse said to me as I slept in the Recovery Room.

"Huh?" I said slowly.

"Wake up, Josh."

"What?" I said. I was confused and didn't know where I was.

"That's it, Joshua, good boy. It's time for you to wake up now, Sweetie, you're all finished," the nurse said.

"I am?" I asked. "Where are my moms?"

"They've been waiting for you. I'll get them right now."

My parents came in to see me. They smiled and kissed me.

"That's quite a bandage you have, Joshie," Momma B said.

"Your head won't get cold this winter with that wrapped around it," Mom said.

I stayed in the recovery room for about two hours and then Dr. Gibbs told my parents they could drive me home. I slept the whole way. I woke up when we pulled into our garage.

Mom helped me walk into the house. I wasn't very steady on my feet.

"I want to go to the bathroom," I said. "I want to see myself in the mirror."

Mom led me to the bathroom and turned on the lights. I was amazed at what I saw.

"Oh, my gosh!" I said. "I look like a giant Q-tip! How long do I have to wear this bandage?"

I wanted to see what my head looked like under the bandage.

"Dr. Gibbs wants to see you in three days," Mom said. "He'll see how well you're healing, and he may change your bandage then."

"Do I have to go back to school looking like this?" I asked.

"No, Sweetheart," Mom said. "Your bandages will be long gone by the time school starts again after the Holidays. You'll just have a thin little scar where your Angel Kiss used to be."

"Sweet," I said. "Can I go back to sleep now?"

"Of course," Mom said.

Three days later we went to see Dr. Gibbs. He was pleased with how I was healing. And just like Mom said, the bandages were all gone by the time school started in January.

"Moms," I said one evening during dinner. "I know that some people don't believe in magic or miracles or Santa Clause, but I do. I know they're real."

"Well, I believe in miracles and Santa Clause," Momma B said.

"Me too!" said my mom.

"Mom, do you remember a few years ago when I talked to Santa at the mall?"

"Yes," Mom said. "You wouldn't tell us what you asked for."

"That's because Santa told me that he couldn't get me what I wanted that year. He said that I'd have to wait a few years for my Christmas wish to come true."

"I remember that," Momma B said. "What was your wish, Joshie?"

"I asked Santa to make my Angel Kiss disappear. I was tired of people always asking about it and teasing me."

"Well, it looks like Santa came through for you," Mom said.

"He sure did," I said nodding my head.

School started again in early January. I was excited about sharing my Christmas story with the teachers and the kids in my class.

When someone asked me if I had a good Christmas or what Santa brought me, I'd smile and turn around to show them the back of my head.

"This year my Christmas was perfect," I said. "I got exactly what I asked Santa for; a normal looking head. Now nobody's going to tease me about my bald spot again."

The End

Jan Crossen

A Note From The Author

The **9 Lives Trilogy** is a fictional series inspired by my adopted son, Joshua. These books are for preteens, teenagers, and adults. My goal is to raise awareness of FASD, and to promote healthy births and healthy, alcohol and drug free babies.

Joshua has permanent brain damage because his birth mother drank alcohol while she was pregnant with him. The alcohol caused him to have a disability known as Fetal Alcohol Spectrum Disorders (FASD). A developing fetus, exposed to even a small amount of alcohol, can suffer permanent brain damage. FASD covers a wide spectrum of developmental, mental, and physical handicaps. A child with FASD may have a normal appearance, and a normal to genius IQ, and still have brain damage. Or he may have obvious physical differences and mental retardation.

Statistics show that 1 out of every 100 babies born in North American has been exposed to alcohol in utero. The number one issue for children, teenagers, and adults with FASD, is behavioral problems.

Individuals with FASD have trouble with money, memory, impulse control, abstract reasoning, and making good decisions. They cannot connect cause and effect, and they do not learn from their mistakes. The person with FASD can recite the rules, but is not able to follow them.

Fetal Alcohol Spectrum Disorders are 100% preventable. Those affected by FASD cut across all social, cultural and economic genres. Sixty percent of all women of childbearing age consume alcohol. Fifty percent of all pregnancies are unplanned. Many women drink alcohol in the early stages of pregnancy, before they realize that they are pregnant. The damage to their developing fetuses may already be done. No amount of alcohol is safe to consume when a woman is pregnant.

I hope that you enjoy the books and that you will share them with others.

Thank you.

Jan Crossen

Resources:

Colorado Cultural Heritage Camps

A weekend camping experience for the entire family, providing positive, ethnic heritage experiences for adopted children.
Camps are available for:
> African/Caribbean
> Cambodian
> Chinese
> Indian/Nepalese
> Filipino
> Korean
> Latin American
> Russian/Eastern European/Central Asian
> Vietnamese

Pam Sweetser, Executive Director
Colorado Cultural Heritage Camps
2052 Elm St.
Denver, CO. 80207
www.heritagecamps.org

Whispering Hope Ranch

WHR is a sanctuary for animals with physical differences or those who have been rescued from difficult situations. It is also a peaceful environment for individuals with special needs, physical or developmental challenges. The animal residents interact with their guests, and the visitors find nurturing and acceptance, as a result of animal to human connection.

Diane Reid, Director
Whispering Hope Ranch
HC2 Box 162-V
Payson, AZ 85541
928-478-0339
www.whisperinghoperanch.org

Fetal Alcohol Spectrum Disorder (FASD)

National Organization on Fetal Alcohol Syndrome
www.nofas.org

FASD State Resource Directory
www.nofas.org/resource/directory

Available Assistance for Individuals with Disabilities
www.nofas.org/living

Special Education Law & Advocacy for Children with
Special Needs www.wrightslaw.com

The Family Empowerment Network
www.pregnancyandalcohol.org

Community Resources & Family Support Groups
www.nofas.org/resource/results.aspx

Fetal Alcohol Syndrome Community Resource Center

Teresa Kellerman, Director
7725 E 33rd St
Tucson, AZ 85710
520-296-9172
www.come-over.to/FAS/Citizen
www.FASSTAR.com

"Iceberg" On-line Newsletter www.fasiceberg.org
ADHD/ADD is often diagnosed with FASD
www.chadd.org

Support networks in each state for families, children, and adults with special needs.
Judd103w@wonder.em.cdc.gov

The ARC has materials about Fetal Alcohol Syndrome.
www.thearc.org

FASD Center for Excellence
http://fasdcenter.samhsa.gov

This ARCH website helps families by listing various options for disabled and children in all 50 states.
www.respitelocator.org/index.htm

Parent support groups in the United States:
http://depts.washington.edu/fadu/Support.Groups.US.html

Parent support groups in Canada:
http://depts.washington.edu/fadu/Support.Groups.CA.html

Fetal Alcohol Syndrome Diagnostic & Prevention Network at the University of Washington
University of Washington Fetal Alcohol Drug Unit

180 Nickerson St, Suite 309
Seattle, WA 98109
206-543-7155
fadu@u.washington.edu
http://depts.washington.edu/fadu/

ADOPTION

North American council on Adoptable Children has information on adoption subsidies, newsletters. www.nacac.org

National Resource Center for Special Needs Adoption offers training and adoption support to families, newsletter. www.spaulding.org

Parent Network for the Post-Institutionalized Child provides technical assistance for adoptions of children from hospitals and orphanages in other countries. www.pnpic.org

National Adoption Center www.adopt.org

Rainbow Kids, Adoption Information, Support www.RainbowKids.com

Adoption Books:
www.emkpress.com

www.tapestrybooks.com

www.adoptionshop.com

www.adoptivefamilies.com

www.comeunity.com

Adoption Week e-magazine
http://e-magazine.adoption.com/

Gay, Lesbian, Transgender Families:

Family Pride http://familypride.ecrater.com

www.familypride.org

Rainbow Families www.rainbowfamilies.org

Human Rights Campaign (HRC)
www.hrc.org/familynet

www.proudparenting.com

www.gayparenting.com

www.andbabymagazine.com

Other Books in the 9 Lives Trilogy:

9 Lives, I Will Survive   Oct 2007

ISBN: 9780979398186 $23.00
Hard Cover with Jacket

ISBN: 9780979398193 $12.25
Soft Cover

Joshua is a tenacious young boy who, like a lucky cat, appears to live a charmed life by defying death on several occasions. His challenges began while he was still in his birth mother's womb. She drank alcohol during her pregnancy with him. This is a story of survival, and the interracial adoption of an older, special needs child into a home with two loving and committed mothers.

9 Lives, Full Circle   **Fall 2008**

The middle and high school years are especially difficult for Joshua. Like most teens, he struggles with his identity. He is handsome and has a normal IQ, yet he has social, academic, and behavioral issues that are hard to explain. These problems lead him down the wrong paths. He reunites with a birth family member, and realizes that he has an invisible disability. Josh must find a way to manage his handicap and achieve his dreams.

Jan Crossen

Printed in the United States
211968BV00004B/4/P